PENGUIN BOOKS

GARTH AND THE MERMAID

Born and raised in Kansas, Barbara Smucker worked as both a researcher and a journalist before marrying Donovan Smucker and moving to Chicago where they raised their three children. In 1969 they moved to Waterloo, Ontario, where Barbara became a children's librarian and went on to write most of her books.

Ms Smucker's many stories for children have won her several awards, including a Canada Council Award, the Ruth Schwartz Award and the Brotherhood Award of the U.S. National Conference of Christians and Jews.

GARTH AND THE MERMAID

Barbara Smucker

Penguin Books

PENGUIN BOOKS

Published by the Penguin Group

Penguin Books Canada Ltd, 10 Alcorn Avenue, Toronto, Ontario, Canada M4V 3B2

Penguin Books Ltd, 27 Wrights Lane, London W8 5TZ, England

Penguin Books USA Inc., 375 Hudson Street, New York, New York 10014, U.S.A.

Penguin Books Australia Ltd, Ringwood, Victoria, Australia

Penguin Books (NZ) Ltd, 182-190 Wairau Road, Auckland 10, New Zealand

Penguin Books Ltd, Registered Offices: Harmondsworth, Middlesex, England

First published in Viking by Penguin Books Canada Limited, 1992

Published in Penguin Books, 1994

1 3 5 7 9 10 8 6 4 2

Publisher's note: This book is a work of fiction. Names, characters, places and incidents either are the product of the author's imagination or are used fictitiously, and any resemblance to actual persons living or dead, events, or locales is entirely coincidental.

Manufactured in Canada

Canadian Cataloguing in Publication Data

Smucker, Barbara, 1915-
Garth and the mermaid

I. Title.

PS8537.M82G37 1994   jC813'.54   C92-094119-2
PZ7.S66Ga 1994

For my daughter Rebecca, who helped me with the research for this book in England

A Note to the Reader

The action in this novel takes place in Canada in the town of Guelph, Ontario, and in an area in southeast England known as East Anglia. The East Anglian village of Dodding and the town of Isle are fictitious.

The events that occur in England are set in medieval times, around 1320. The characters—the peasants, the stone carvers, the holy men of the Benedictine Priory of Isle—are my inventions, but I have attempted to make them as historically accurate as possible.

The inspiration for the story came from a visit I made to Ely Cathedral several years ago: a guide pointed to a small sculpture of a mermaid and said it appeared to have been carved by an apprentice, even though apprentices weren't normally allowed to work on carvings in the cathedral. That started me thinking . . .

GARTH
AND THE
MERMAID

❧ 1 ❧

It was near midnight when the university chorus ended their concert in the high-ceilinged Gothic cathedral that towered above the town of Guelph. The clear notes of the sopranos seemed to linger among the tall columns. The warm stillness of June circled the building like protecting arms.

Garth Merriman and his best friend, Ed, strolled out through the open doors of the Church of Our Lady with the crowd of listeners. Garth took a full deep breath. The air was delicious. It was like breathing the fragrance of ripe grapes.

"I could explode," he gasped dramatically to his friend, "with all this great singing and all this good air inside me. I think the buttons on this stupid new shirt might pop."

Tall, husky Garth and the smaller Ed strode like opera singers down the steps of the hill that sloped down from the cathedral.

Garth completely forgot that he was supposed to wait inside for his mother and Hawk Goderich, the dour-faced man who was soon to become his stepfather. On a night like this, he refused to think about the painful subject of the coming marriage. Still it was Hawk who had bought him the new clothes he was wearing tonight.

The music, the star-filled summer sky, and the medieval splendour of the church seemed to lift the two boys off the ground and blow them into a make-believe world. It didn't matter for the moment that Garth's new clothes were stiff and uncomfortable, or that Ed's jeans were frayed, or that a bandage covering a cut on his forehead was hideously dirty. Both boys were in a crazy, jubilant mood.

They jumped over the low stone wall that skirted the steps and onto the steep lawn and began sliding down it. Garth's ill-fitting new shoes skidded and he rolled into a somersault. Both boys landed at the bottom in a convulsion of laughter.

"Kneel before me, Garth!" Ed cried as he flourished a fallen tree branch. "With this sword, I, John LeMaine, lord of the manor of Dodding, dub thee awkward knight and a carver of stone."

The medieval spire on the Church of Our Lady was a fitting backdrop for their gallant farce. Garth, lying dishevelled in the grass, lifted a shoeless foot.

Pretending to live in the Middle Ages had become a constant game with the two of them. It had started when Ms. Grove had announced the project in their grade-seven history class.

"We'll spend two hours every afternoon living in fourteenth-century England." Her voice rose with excitement. "Each of you will choose to be a knight, a pilgrim, a lord of the manor, a queen, a lady of the manor, a nun—someone who lived during the Middle Ages. Then you'll write a paper on your way of life and make something to represent your new personality."

Voices buzzed. Students conferred with one another. Decisions were made.

"We want to be knights," many of the boys announced.

"A pilgrim," one boy said.

"A queen," several girls decided.

Garth whispered to Ed, who sat behind him. They nodded together and raised their hands.

"I'll be a stone carver in a cathedral," Garth said. "I want to build something that will last a thousand years."

"A stone carver? Weird!" said one boy.

"I'll be a minstrel and sing a song about Robin Hood," Ed laughed. "I'll help Garth build his cathedral."

The last hand rose slowly at the back of the room. It was mysterious Mary Stonehedge, Garth noticed. He thought she was the most beautiful girl in the school. Her dark hair flowed about her head, her eyes sparkled like stars when she talked.

"I want to be a mermaid," she whispered.

"A mermaid?" Ms. Grove was intrigued.

Hisses and mocking laughter could be heard.

"Yeah!" Garth spoke up in Mary's defence. "A lot of people in the Middle Ages believed in supernatural beings like mermaids. They were supposed to reveal things that were about to happen—like storms at sea. They could even learn to live on the land. Mary can live in the ocean near my cathedral."

From that moment Mary became "Mermaid" to everyone but Ms. Grove. And Mary seemed to like her new name.

The school project roared into action. Steel armour and swords were shaped from aluminum foil. Discarded sheets and curtains became elegant gowns for the ladies.

Garth and Ed's cathedral had to be built of cardboard instead of stone. Its tall spire constantly toppled until the boys learned about a flying buttress that would prop it up. They gave their cathedral a name—Isle Cathedral—and they picked an exact date for its completion—1322.

Beautiful, mysterious Mary fashioned a costume that turned her into a mermaid.

Unknown to his teacher and to all of his classmates but Ed, Garth's keen interest in the Middle Ages came from stories he'd heard about his father, who died when he was only two.

Mum didn't talk about him much, but Garth knew that she and his dad had immigrated to Canada from England, where he had worked as a restorer of ancient cathedrals and dreamed of becoming a sculptor of stone.

Once, Garth heard his mother say to a friend, "When Tom and I moved to Canada, we chose Guelph as the place to live. With its warm-coloured, locally quarried limestone, it seemed just right to Tom for his stone carving."

Garth also knew that the Gothic cathedral, with its stone carvings, pointed arches, and tall pillars, standing on top of Guelph's highest hill, had impressed his dad.

Now, at the foot of this hill, Garth and Ed tussled briefly, Garth slipped a white shoe over one hand, fashioning a macabre, flapping glove. As he did so a cruising station wagon skidded to a stop on the street beside him.

"Garth!" a disapproving voice shouted.

Garth looked up. It was Hawk Goderich. Mum was sitting beside him.

Garth froze. Ed seemed to crumple.

The two boys crawled silently into the back seat of the car. Garth noticed that his shirt was covered with grass stains and that his shoes were smudged with mud. He decided that he didn't care.

As they drove along and no one talked, a memory began drumming in Garth's head. It was about the evening Mum had told him she was going to marry Hawk.

Hawk Goderich owned the exclusive furniture store where Garth's mother had a good-paying job as business manager. She liked her work and often talked about her boss. One day she told Garth that she had been to his house.

"It's perfect," she said. "It was like walking through the display rooms of the store."

"Who wants to live in a furniture store?" Garth laughed.

Then Mum put her hand over Garth's strong, slender fingers. "Garth—he's asked me to marry him," she said quietly. "And I've said yes."

"No!" Garth wanted to shout. But the quiet contentment on his mother's face silenced him. He felt squeezed in and alone. It wasn't that he wanted to hang onto Mum like a baby, but there was something about sharing her with Hawk Goderich that bothered him.

Garth winced when he compared this proper, sullen, hard-working man with the image he had of his father.

"I know Hawk can't replace your father," Mum had said. "He was kind and so much fun. He was a dreamer but he didn't live long enough to fulfil those dreams."

That night Mum gave Garth a small chisel that his father had used for his carving, and it became his most treasured possession.

"It's a link with the past for you, Garth, and a hope for the future."

Garth always carried the chisel in the pocket of his pants. He grabbed it now as Hawk glided the car down the dark highway towards the edge of town where he lived. When they reached a small side road, Hawk slowed the car to a smooth stop.

"I think this is where Ed lives," he said abruptly.

Ed swung the car door open and disappeared into the night.

The car hummed again into action.

"It's too bad such a bright boy has to live on a run-down pig farm," Hawk said to Mum.

Garth wanted to cry out, "It's fun being at Ed's house, and it isn't run down." But he remained silent, gripping his small chisel more tightly.

Soon they turned onto Dodding Road, where Hawk's old grey stone house, surrounded by a high wall, rose above the trees. "We'll stop here a minute and then I'll take the two of you home," he said.

A truck driver honked his horn behind them. He was trying to pass Hawk's car and turn into the driveway of the house across the road. Everyone's attention swung in the opposite direction, where a young girl with flowing black hair was streaking down her driveway on a skateboard.

"It's Mermaid!" Garth shouted. "I didn't know she lived here."

Hawk fumed. "It's that Stonehedge girl. What does she mean skateboarding at this hour of the night?"

The trucker honked again. He was heading for the Stonehedges' driveway.

Garth screamed. "Mermaid can't see the

truck! She'll be hit!" He pushed open the car door and jumped out.

"Garth—be careful!" his mother cried out as she scrambled to get out of the car.

The truck brakes screeched. As if everything were happening in slow motion, Garth saw the truck bearing down on him. There was a spray of shattered lights, or was it glass?

Then a thudding darkness struck Garth. He could see nothing. Somewhere in the distance he thought he heard a shrill siren. He felt his mother's hand holding his. He could smell strange antiseptic odours.

There was the sound of wheels rolling beneath him, then the swishing of an elevator that went down, down, down. It seemed to Garth that it was tunnelling into the middle of the earth, taking him farther and farther from home.

🐚 2 🐚

A thick fog seemed to envelop the elevator and billow over Garth. He saw dim, swaying figures: Mum . . . Hawk . . . Mermaid. He tried to reach out to them, but his hands hit endless white clouds of sheets.

The elevator continued to plunge down and down. The vaporous mass shifted soundlessly, then spun into a tunnel of fog closing in around Garth. It seemed to be pulling him, hurtling him through space. He cried out in fear.

The elevator stopped. Wheels began to roll beneath him again. His hands moved to a blanket that now covered him. Why was it mud-soaked and dirty? Bells began to clang. Their ring was strange and yet familiar.

"Wake up Garth, wake up," Garth heard his mother pleading, but her voice was as far away as the end of an echo. Yet she was in the same room with him. He could see her sitting in a dark corner.

She came to him finally, as though she were floating across the room.

"Hurry, Garth," she said. "The parish church

bells are ringing the hour for early morning mass."

"Parish church?" Garth tried to lift himself free from the swirling fog. But he could only lie still under the heavy mantle. It was well that he did, for a human cry pierced the early morning calm. It silenced the bells and shattered the fog into splinters of . . . glass?

"Devils and witches!" Garth heard himself shout. Or *was* it his voice? Everything was odd and yet familiar, as if the fog had sliced through him, making two Garths—one who spoke and one who listened.

The part of him who spoke finally sat upright and flung off the mantle onto a hard earth floor. This Garth wore a tunic of coarse wool and his feet were bare. The packed earth beneath him was the floor of a hut made of wattle (interwoven sticks and twigs) and plaster, with a thatching of straw hanging stiffly from its roof.

Garth's mind whirled and spun.

"Where am I?" he asked.

"Why, home at Dodding," his mother laughed.

Places, dates, and people began to collide, one into the other. Then out of the jumble came a date—1321; a place—the village of Dodding; and a country—England. The Garth who spoke was a peasant boy in the village of Dodding.

The other Garth, the one who listened, dissolved into a wisp of cloud and slipped out through the hole in the roof of the hut. The speaking Garth tried to grasp the disappearing figure, but he slipped through his fingers. Garth rubbed his cheeks. The swelling was gone.

"Open the door! Let in the light!" the peasant boy cried.

Garth's shouts stirred the animals in a stable room next to the hut, and a squealing pig bounded in zig-zags across the floor against his bare legs.

"Garth!" a rasping voice silenced him. "If there are witches in the village of Dodding I will silence them. Now hold your tongue. I will open the door."

It was the crackling voice of his stepfather, Goderic, but he seemed to be suddenly smaller and darker as he stumbled across the room towards the door.

Garth snatched his mantle and felt for the chisel that he always carried under his belt. It was strangely warm, as though heated by an inner flame. Garth clasped it tightly as he backed against the wall of the hut.

He knew that Goderic would scold him soundly for this disturbance. In the dim light he saw his stepfather in a wool shirt and tunic, standing hunched against the morning chill.

"A gnarled and twisted oak," he mumbled, glancing at Goderic's twisted mouth and shaggy black brows. Garth was puzzled again by the change in Goderic's appearance. Usually there was no warmth for Garth from this man he must now call Father. But this morning hunched Goderic seemed to view him with worry and concern.

Garth fingered the chisel again. It was a comfort, somehow, to know that this small tool had once belonged to his real father.

For a second this knowledge startled Garth. But as he tried to hold onto the thought, his head seemed to fill with cobwebs. Then, a surprising fragrance of purple grapes cleansed the air as well as his head. He looked around. Yes, he belonged here.

Outside the door of the hut a bent figure stepped through the silent fog, trudging along the footpath to the church. It was Wat, their neighbour.

"It will be known at the church what the strange cry is about, Goderic," he called out.

"That it will," Goderic rasped.

By now Mother had coaxed the pig back into the stable room. She shook the wrinkled apron over her thick woollen kirtle and drew it tightly about her waist with a girdle of hemp. Wisps of yellow hair were swiftly tucked beneath her headkerchief. Garth glanced at her quickly. This was his mother, and yet something about her was different.

He swiftly put this puzzling thought aside when he saw that Mother sensed the impatience of Goderic and the uneasiness of all of them about the strange cry. She was setting about to quiet them.

"Pour the ale, Garth," she said softly, coming to him and running her fingers quickly through his tangled yellow curls.

Carefully she broke three chunks of bread from a rye loaf and handed one to each of them. The largest piece went to Goderic.

"We must go at once to the church," Goderic said, munching the bread between gulps of ale.

Time was not wasted in dressing, for Garth and his family, like the other peasants of Dodding, slept in the brown, dirty clothes they wore during the day. Each of them considered themselves lucky to have a second tunic or kirtle to wear for the harvest festival that would soon be upon them. Since it was still summer, there was no need for shoes, though they wore long leggings.

Garth watched the gentle outline of Mother's face. There would be no scolding now. Goderic was impatient to be on his way.

With Goderic in the lead, the family set off down the footpath to the church. The huts of their neighbours were now hidden by fog, but the top of the church tower, with its wooden spire, had pierced the mist and appeared to float unattached over the hill.

Beyond it, on another hill, the grey stone manor house of Sir John LeMaine loomed stark and aloof, as though the guards of the high stone wall around it had forbidden the fog to enter.

As Garth and his family crossed the damp turf of the village green near the church, the shrill words of John the smith rose to greet them.

"They seized Edmund, the son of Egbert the swineherd, and brought him to my shop before dawn."

"Edmund!" Garth cupped his hand over his mouth to stifle a cry. They had found Edmund, his best and closest friend, who had run away only a fortnight ago. Why had they taken him to the blacksmith's shop? Could the cry have come from his punishment?

"A peasant boy should know better than to run away," Goderic muttered.

Thomas the stone carver intervened. "Hawkin did beat him unduly the night before he escaped."

"Hawkin?" For a confused moment Garth's head began spinning again as though searching for a memory that kept racing away from him. He grabbed his chisel. It steadied him, and slowly the village of Dodding came back into focus.

Now he remembered. Sir John LeMaine was gone from the manor house. At such a time his cruel steward, Hawkin, ruled the peasants with an iron hand. He had beat Edmund unduly just as Thomas said.

Edmund's running away had been a fearful thing for the peasants.

"He will be murdered by robbers," some of them whispered.

"He will die from the beating," Edmund's father moaned.

And each morning, without telling anyone, Garth prayed fervently in the church that Edmund was alive and that he was somehow living in Isle, near the great cathedral there.

Often he and Edmund had heard tales of Isle Cathedral from pilgrims who trudged along the footpath through Dodding. The two boys dreamed of going there together someday.

Garth crowded near the men who stood about the yew tree in the churchyard. John the smith was talking.

"A knight from our manor found Edmund at the Priory of Isle begging food from the monks. Steward Hawkin brought him to my place this morning to be punished. He ordered him to be branded on the forehead."

There were cries of horror and surprise among the peasants.

"If Sir John were at home he would not have punished him thus!" Garth cried.

Garth searched for Thomas the stone carver. Only Thomas and Mother would understand his frantic concern about Edmund. Thomas had been in Dodding only a year, coming at the bidding of Sir John to make new carvings for the parish church. Almost at once Garth found him to be a friend. Surely his own father must have been the image of Thomas.

Now Thomas slumped against the yew trunk, his face drained of colour. Garth walked to his side.

"I was the one who told him about running away. How could I, Garth?" Thomas spoke softly to keep others from hearing.

For Garth the memory was like a bad dream. He and Edmund had escaped for a moment from their work in the fields. They were eager to watch Thomas carve figures above the church door and hear his tales of travelling in other towns and cities. Thomas had said to them, half chiding, "If you want to be stone carvers and travellers, my lads, you will have to be free men. And the only way the two of you will ever be free is to run away from this village and not be found for a year and a day."

"Stone carvers?" Garth had thrilled at the words. There was nothing in his life he wanted more to be.

"A year and a day?" he had asked.

"It's a law," Thomas had said, "and—"

But Thomas's words had been cut short, for Hawkin swept down upon them, hitting Edmund with a sharp rod and knocking him to the ground.

"I'll teach you not to leave your work," he had cried.

That night, Edmund had disappeared.

"I'm going to Edmund now," Garth whispered to Thomas.

Thomas grabbed Garth's hand and pulled him towards the church. "You will anger your father and miss the mass. You can see Edmund later."

3

Garth stumbled into the church. Misery wrapped around him like a cloak. Usually the grey stone pillars and the quiet nave were a comfort to him. This morning he hardly noticed them. He found a place against the wall of the church and stood with the other peasants waiting for the service to begin. He saw his mother wipe tears from her eyes. Edmund was like another son to her. As soon as the service ended, he would go to Edmund. Now he mumbled a silent prayer for his friend.

Edmund had taken hard blows before, Garth thought. Surely he would recover from this one.

Two cabbages and some leeks rolled out from under a stone bench. Garth knew that they had been brought by someone for the priest's tithe barn, yet he eyed them hungrily. The cooking pots of the peasants of Dodding were often nearly empty just before the harvest.

Garth knew that in his cottage there was rye for only two more loaves of bread, a few leeks, and some cabbages in the croft. That was all. Even the ale was weak with water added from the river.

17

Garth's thoughts wandered briefly from Edmund to the aching hunger inside him. He vowed to himself that he would poach a rabbit in the manor forests soon. He did not like to take what was not rightfully his, for the peasants were forbidden to hunt in the forest of Sir John LeMaine. But even dour Goderic, who usually obeyed every law demanded by the lord of his peasants, was sometimes driven to poaching when the cooking pot held nothing at all.

Garth glanced quickly at his stepfather standing against the wall. He thought of how Goderic seldom caused trouble for Sir John or even for Steward Hawkin, and how he did provide shelter for him and his mother. But always foremost in his mind were the words his stepfather uttered over and over like the pounding of a mallet:

"I paid the death fee for my wife's first husband. And I took her bungling son, Garth, in the bargain."

He was a bungler, Garth knew, and he sometimes stopped his work in the fields when he found a soft stone to carve with his chisel. But he did try to help Goderic, if only for Mother's sake.

Was his real father called a bungler, too? Garth wondered, rubbing his fingers over the small chisel.

"It's a link with the past and a hope for the future."

Garth tensed. These strange words came into his head as though they belonged there. Who would have said them? He glanced around the church, then shook his head to drive the strange words away.

Near him stood Egbert the swineherd, Edmund's father. He had withdrawn into the folds of his mantle.

Edmund is alone in his hut, Garth realized. I will run to him as soon as the service ends.

On most mornings, the time of mass was a peaceful moment in Garth's hard-working day. No one shouted commands at him inside the church. He liked watching the sunlight pour through the stained-glass window. Pools of red, blue, and gold splashed like magic over the round pillars and onto the face of St. Peter, whose brightly painted carved figure stood near the east wall.

Sometimes, during early mass, Garth would dream of carving a head for one of the beautifully decorated arches over the doorway, as Thomas did. He pictured himself using his small chisel and a mallet to shape the face of a saint. He would work day and night to please God.

But Garth would tear out his tongue before telling this dream to anyone. No peasant ever became a stone carver. A man with a craft like carving must be a free man and freedom must be bought. Garth had never held a coin in his hand. He didn't dare to think of following Thomas and his advice to escape for a year and a day. Edmund had tried and now he would forever bear a scar

on his forehead. Yet Garth had to admit that
Edmund *had* reached Isle, and he envied him
that.

Goderic and many of the other peasants of
Dodding scoffed at Garth's chipping away at
stone.

"A hulk of a boy like you with the strength of
an ox," Goderic often cried out when he caught
him at it. "Why must you waste your time at such a
useless task?"

But, in spite of the buffets from all of them,
Garth could not forget his dream. And it was this
dream that made the scoffs and cuffings bearable.

Suddenly the west door of the church opened
and all eyes shifted towards it. Sir John's wife, Lady
Margaret, was arriving with her attendants. They
swept down the centre of the nave towards the
chancel to stand with Walter the priest. The peasant women huddled at the back of the nave bent
forward to stare at the fine dresses of the ladies.
The men shuffled their feet with impatience at
this delay in the service. They needed to make use
of the daylight hours in the fields.

Sunlight sparkled on Lady Margaret's gold-
and-silver cotte of thick brocade. It shone on her
pale face, outlined with a white wimple that covered all her hair.

Garth and the other peasant boys were more
interested in the hooded goshawk that perched
on the wrist of the attendant of young Agnes, the
daughter of Lady Margaret and Sir John. Garth

knew that the hawk was in training for the coming hunt and that it must learn to be among people.

The face of Walter the priest twisted with distaste. He could not abide hawks in the church. The peasant boys began to whisper and jest. And even though the priest believed that the salvation of a peasant was just as important as that of a nobleman, the whispering made him angry. He smote his hand on the open missal at the altar and bid all of them keep their silence.

Hawkin the steward wheeled about. He was taller than most of those about him and the elegance of his clothing outdid even that of the ladies. His deep blue surcoat spread wide like the wings of a swan. It was just as white inside, for the lining was of fur. Flat brown hair framed his long, pinched face.

The fringed bangs across his forehead touched his fierce eyebrows. And his eyes were cold, dark, and narrow, as though he were peering through the slits of a helmet. Garth started when Hawkin shifted his gaze and looked straight at him.

Was Hawkin remembering the beating of Edmund before he ran away and how Garth, too, had missed his work to watch Thomas carve?

🐚 4 🐚

At last the service ended. Garth hurried towards the door. Outside, golden sunlight had broken through the fog, sending it in smoke-like tufts over the battlements of the manor house. Traces of the fog drifted above the common fields of ripe grain and stretched into the waste and woodlands. To Garth, the sunshine brought no joy. A black day with foreboding winds would have better fit his mood.

He tried to dodge the eyes of Goderic by ducking behind the heavy-needled branches of the yew. But Goderic was wary.

"Aye there, Garth," he called. "Don't be looking for an escape. The pigs must go to the forest and the sickle must be sharpened for the harvest."

This was what Garth wanted—to be told to take the pigs to the forest! The sickle could wait. He would hurry the animals along and turn them over to Edmund's father, Egbert, who cared for all the pigs of the village during the day.

Garth ran down the path that led to his hut. Over his shoulder he could see the deep blue surcoat of Hawkin swinging in the wind as he escorted the ladies back to the manor house.

"I'll need a sharp stick to prod those slow-moving beasts," Garth said to himself. He thought of the tools that hung along their cottage wall. They were his stepfather's pride—the hoe, the sickle, the spade, the axe, the pruning hook. The pruning hook would be perfect for his needs. Its sharp curved end, which could slice dead branches from their twisted apple tree and trim their hedge in spring, would make the two pigs squeal.

Goderic would never use this tool for such a purpose, and Garth knew that he must guard the pruning hook with his life. But at the moment one thought blotted out all caution. He could not wait to see Edmund.

Garth reached his own hut as a patch of sunlight spread over it, giving the wattle and plaster of which it was made a warm, pink glow. His head brushed the overhanging eaves of thatch and he reminded himself that he should help Goderic trim it.

He backed away to give the thatch an upward push and kicked the iron cooking pot behind him, sending it swinging on its trivet and spilling drops of soup from right to left.

"A blundering fool I am indeed," Garth thought and bent to steady the pot and look inside. There would be only one bowl for each of them tonight. Garth's stomach ached again with hunger.

"In the name of good St. Benedict, I will poach a rabbit for tonight and toss it in the soup," he vowed aloud.

He knew, however, as did the other peasants of Dodding, that if he were caught stealing a rabbit from the lord's forest the lightest punishment would be a day in the pillory with his neck and hands sticking through the holes. Sometimes Sir John looked the other way on the lean days before harvest. He might even pretend not to notice if fish were caught in his river or one of his pigeons pelted down for winging too far from the dovecote. But it went against Garth's nature to hide his deeds. Why should he be driven to stealing when the forest fairly leaped with rabbits and the pond jumped with fish?

Steward Hawkin was different. A theft under his sharp nose—even if the victim were pale with hunger—met the leash and the pillory.

Thinking of Hawkin was reason for an uneasy glance at the manor house, surrounded by its high stone wall, where Garth hoped Lady Margaret was still keeping him busy.

Usually Garth's cheerful, blustering mood concealed the tears and bruises of the day, but his misery about Edmund hurt him deep inside. He could not laugh this day, and sometimes his eyes smarted with tears.

He lifted the pruning hook from the wall, vowing not to lose it and to return it at once. The bony pigs were by now grunting and nudging against the wall of the stable attached to the cottage. They needed but one prod to send them trotting down the path to the woods where they would spend the day grubbing for acorns and roots.

On such a fine day, with the sun warming his face, Garth would ordinarily have idled the pigs and stopped for a chat with one of the neighbours along the footpath. Or he might have ducked onto the path into the forest beyond the swineherd's hut and tried to see the castle of Earl Robert de Lindsay. Sir John held his manor from the Earl.

None of the peasants of Dodding had seen the castle and none of them planned to—least of all Goderic. But a devil gnawed at Garth's bones and made him wish for the sights of other places.

Today, though, he did not loiter. He prodded the pigs with such force that one of them stumbled into a bank of thick rushes and had to be pushed to right itself on its four spindly legs.

By now the other swine of the village were being gathered on the fringe of the forest to be watched by Egbert the swineherd. Garth shoved his pigs into the midst of them and hurried to Edmund's hut.

The hut was caved in at one end and the thatch on the roof, for lack of fresh straw, was as stiff as wood. A gnarled apple tree, mantled with ivy, choked the entrance to the hut and gave such thick shade that there was no light inside even with the door swung wide open. This morning the door was closed.

Garth saw thin smoke drift from the hole in the roof.

"It's Garth. I've come to see you!" he shouted.

There was a stir inside. Setting down the pruning hook, Garth pushed the door open. A feeble fire smouldered on the flat stone hearth in the centre of the room. The smoke that hung in the air made Garth cough.

He looked towards the corner where he knew Edmund slept. At first all he could see were the folds of a tattered mud-brown mantle and the scatterings of loose straw from a pallet. He stepped closer. Just then the fire caught some straw and sprayed the hut with light. Edmund lay sleeping, his face swollen and bruised.

Edmund stirred and his eyes opened. He recognized his friend, for he raised a feeble hand, but he couldn't speak.

Garth's bungling manner possessed him. "Mother will come and bathe your head and bring her healing herbs, Edmund. I will bring you food. I will fill your empty cooking pot with meat if I must throw stones at all the pigeons in the dovecote!"

Edmund tried to smile. Garth took off his own mantle and gently covered his friend. He could wear that old mantle that Goderic had discarded.

"You made the trip to Isle, Edmund." Garth bent close to his friend. There was admiration in his voice. Then he whirled about the room, jerking tight the grass rope girdle that held in the folds of his tunic.

"If you have good food, Edmund, you will get better," he shouted again. He ran from the hut, forgetting the treasured pruning hook.

❦ 5 ❦

Garth ran breathlessly back to his hut. He hoped that Mother would be there milking the cow, which they kept in the stable room with the pigs. She would waste no time going to Edmund, Garth was certain. And she would not tell Goderic.

Goderic would fuss and fume that a peasant who broke the rules of his lord deserved to be punished. Garth could not accept this rigid thinking. Sometimes when he said what he thought he was accused of having devilish and strange ideas. Garth did not know where they came from. No one else but Edmund and sometimes Mother ever seemed to agree with him.

But Garth did have to admit that in spite of Goderic's sour and stubborn nature he had good qualities. He had the best-tended strips of grain in the common fields, the lands the peasants rented from Sir John. The rents were not paid in coins, because the peasants had almost none, but they worked three days each week on Sir John's estate and gave him part of the harvests from their own

strips as well. Goderic's family ate better than
some, because of his dogged work.

Garth called loudly for Mother, but there was
no answer. He would have to search for her later.
He knew he was needed in the fields, especially
with the coming harvest, but Edmund's care came
first. He would fill the empty iron cooking pot
that hung under the stiff eaves of the swineherd's
hut and have some left over for their own.

Garth thought of snaring rabbits and pigeons
and perhaps a fish or two from the river that
flowed through the village. Of all of these, catching a fish seemed the fastest and best thing to do.

As Garth reached the nearest field, he saw
Goderic. He was hunched over, working in his
strip of ripening grain. Garth scrambled behind a
bramble bush and waited. His stepfather stood up,
scanning the manor house and the green beyond.

"He wonders why I don't come to work,"
Garth thought. He ran down to the base of the
turreted stone wall that surrounded the manor
house. Once there, he crept close to the wall,
grateful for the covering of a small alder tree. At
the turn of the wall, he dodged away from it towards the hut of John the smith.

He did not want to be seen here. John's nim-
ble tongue was never silent and he could do both
good and harm to a person in the same breath.
Garth raced behind the hut and headed for the
common pasture. The ambling cows did not lift
their heads.

A jump across the footpath leading to Isle, the well-trodden road where travellers came and went through Dodding, and Garth was at the bank of the placid River Dodding.

He searched the rushes for a net which he and Edmund kept in a secret place. It was stiff and mouldy from lack of use, but it worked. Garth swished it through the water and was preparing to plunge it in for a catch when he heard the sound of hoofbeats, the yelping of dogs, and the shouts of a hunting party. The hunters were beside him before he could scramble away.

The hunting dogs bounded in and out of the rushes near the water, flushing up honking coots. Young Agnes, the proud daughter of Sir John, sat astride her pony a short way up the slope. The hooded goshawk was poised on her wrist. Garth was surrounded by a hawking party! The chief falconer rode into view among the crowd of grooms.

They had not seen Garth yet. Perhaps if he sat still without moving his head, they would pass by. He held his breath as a coot sailed into the sky. He saw Agnes prepare to cast off her goshawk in pursuit of it. Garth leaned forward to watch, for the hawk would soon head straight for its victim and there would be a wild chase by everyone to keep in view of the kill and lure the hawk back.

Suddenly Garth's bare feet slipped and he fell down the muddy bank. He splashed feet first into the water. The hunters stopped. Agnes looked down at Garth over the green folds of her thick brocaded cloak. Her light brown hair, held back by a chaplet of fresh red poppies, blew about her shoulders. Garth was stunned by the closeness of her beauty, but her eyes were filled with scorn and disapproval. She said in a brittle voice, "This boy is the peasant who bungles so much. Now he is stealing fish in my father's river. He must be punish—" She didn't finish her sentence, for a cry from the falconer interrupted.

"Unhood the hawk!" he shouted.

Garth looked up. The coot had changed its course and was now directly above them. Agnes lifted the goshawk's hood and unclasped the chain on his leg that held him to her wrist. In an instant, the bird sailed upward and was soon trailing the coot, almost as though he were tied to his prey with a small grass rope.

Agnes nudged her pony and galloped with the hunting party into the lord of the manor's forest. Garth knew that they must be present for the kill, or the coot and the goshawk might both be lost.

Garth steadied himself by grasping the branch of an overhanging willow. He wanted to run from the scene and forget the fish, but concern for Edmund and anger at Agnes made him stay. He reached for the net and carefully pulled it through the water. It came to the surface, empty. He tried again. A sudden jerk and the net almost slipped from his hands. He braced himself against the willow branch and tugged at the net, twisting it around and around to close the opening.

"It tosses about as if there were fifty fish inside," he thought.

With one hand he grabbed the branch and pulled himself to the grass-covered bank. The net tossed and splashed behind him.

"I'll not lose it now," Garth laughed. He liked this tugging battle. Agnes was not the only one hunting. He had captured a prey that must be six times bigger than a simple coot.

He pulled slowly and steadily. The net slipped over the bank onto the grass. The writhing creature inside twisted and turned in all directions.

"An eel!" Garth shouted in spite of the need to hide himself and his catch.

But the hunting party had disappeared. Garth began dragging the slithering eel towards his hut. Mother would help him kill it and divide the flesh so a portion could be taken to Edmund. To have eel in the soup kettle would be a rare and delicious treat. And nothing could be better to fill Edmund's empty stomach.

It was good that Garth's cottage was the one nearest the river. A quick run across the pasture and he was there. It took both his hands to steady the net and twist it more tightly about the jerking eel. His dripping, dirt-stained tunic sent streams of muddy water down his legs and over his bare feet.

Mother was outside the hut piling sticks and brush for winter fuel. She looked up at Garth's approach. When she saw the eel in the dripping fishing net, she turned pale.

"It is a good catch, Garth." She motioned him into the hut and then closed the door. "But it will mean trouble for you and for those of us who eat it."

Garth had no time for worry. He was needed in the common fields. Already Goderic was probably in a rage, calling him a sloth as well as a bungler.

"I caught it for Edmund," he gasped, finding himself breathless. "He has nothing to eat, Mother. Please take half of it to him and put the other half into our kettle. No one will report us at this time of year, when all of us are hollow with hunger."

"No, not even Goderic," Mother agreed. "But what of Edmund?"

Garth told her quickly of the swollen face and the fitful fever that sent Edmund tossing and turning on his scattered straw pallet. He told her, too, of covering Edmund with his mantle. He was careful, however, not to mention one word of his encounter with Agnes.

Mother's gentle face became tight with anger. "It is good that you went to Edmund, Garth. I will take some of the eel to him quickly and a potion to heal the wound." She paced busily around the small hut. "And I will take an old mantle of Goderic's. You must have your own mantle, Garth, or you will die of cold." She looked at him solemnly. "You know, Garth, I am like you. I cannot always abide the rules of Sir John for his peasants."

Garth was reassured. Mother would see that Edmund was cared for. Now, if only he could dodge Hawkin and still the anger of Goderic with whispered promises of a delicious soup with eel in it.

Garth brushed against the tools hanging on the wall. Because of the dim light, he felt with his hand to avoid banging into them. An unfamiliar empty space stretched between the spade and the axe. Suddenly he remembered—the pruning hook! He had left it on the ground outside Edmund's hut. Goderic would explode with anger. He would have to get it at all costs before Goderic discovered its loss. He quickly shifted the tools and filled the empty space.

Outside the sun shone strong and warm. Under it, the meadow was bright green and the placid River Dodding uncoiled like a blue snake along its edge. The smell of ripe grain weighted the windless air. To Garth's nose it had already become the smell of baking loaves. Worries and fears faded a little from his mind.

It would soon be the joyous time of Lammas, one of the best holidays of the year for the peasants. All of them and many of the craftsmen of the village harvested Sir John's demesne and the common fields together. There would be dancing and singing and games on the green. Best of all, Sir

John would give a feast in the open court of the manor.

As Garth passed the doorway of John the smith, he heard him say that grain for the Lammas loaf of bread would be reaped in a sunny corner of the lord's demesne at noon! The baker had already fired his oven to bake it. If the Lammas loaf appeared on the altar at Sunday mass it would mean that grain was ready for harvest. Then reaping would begin on Monday and the villagers would be certain of food.

A bright thought gladdened Garth's mind. Perhaps the news of Lammas would make the hawking party forget his splash into the river. At least they had not seen the eel.

Garth approached the middle field, gold with ripe barley, which later would be brewed into ale. He saw Goderic bent over, weeding in a far corner.

"I will work here," Garth decided quickly, "and miss his sharp tongue." He joined in the clearing of sticks and stones from the rough balks that ran between all the strips. There must be no obstacles when the reapers moved through the fields with their sickles for the harvest.

At the same instant a black cloud circled over him. Beyond it, the sun still shone. But the circle of black was a thing apart. It had a chill about it. Garth rose slowly. A raw voice snapped out at him.

"Garth Merriman! You were seen fishing on the lord's estate."

Out of the corner of his eye, Garth saw the deep blue surcoat of Steward Hawkin.

Just then a trumpet blared in the distance and a voice called loudly, "Sir John has returned!"

Hawkin turned about and hastened towards the manor house. The rod which he had been holding over Garth fell to the ground. Garth kicked it away with relief and anger. But he had no time to speak. John the smith walked by, talking loudly to a companion.

"King Edward finally went to war to defend the honour of Queen Isabella at Leeds Castle, and Sir John and his knights helped with the victory."

Garth felt no thrill or triumph over the battle. The knights always seemed to be at war. But victory for Sir John would be celebrated joyfully at the manor house. Surely in the midst of it no one, not even Hawkin, would remember one peasant boy who had fished in the forbidden river.

6

The afternoon was hard and long for Garth and it did not end until sunset. It was the time not only to prepare for the harvest but also for boon work—extra work done for the lord of the manor at harvest and planting time. Soon they would reap the grain with their sickles, bind it into sheaves, pile them high in carts, and haul them to the lord's barn. Garth's back ached and he felt sodden with the sweat of his labour. When the blessed darkness came, he trudged back to his hut behind Goderic, who was even more hunched over than usual.

They found Mother standing over a small fire, stirring the cooking pot with vigour. She smiled a greeting and then served each of them a bowl of thick soup with eel. For the first time in many days there was contentment among them. Goderic asked no questions. He would never have caught the eel himself, but he ate his portion like a starving man and then gave Garth a sly look of approval. He washed down the last drop of soup with a mug of watered ale and then walked up the lane to talk with his neighbour Wat.

Mother turned to Garth. "With food so scant and starvation so near before the harvest, son, most of our neighbours are also poaching food." She lowered her voice. "Without the eel and a cabbage from our croft, Edmund and his father would be eating nothing but acorns from the forest."

A haunting look of fear and sadness came to Mother's eyes. She continued to talk. "I have heard tales of many hardships at the beginning of the harvest," she said. "There is the story of the year an invading army rode into Dodding. They stole our ripened grain, burned our cottages and killed everyone in their path. . . . Our knights were gone, fighting other wars."

Garth knew that part of the peasant's pay was protection by the knights of Sir John. But he found himself wondering sometimes about these favoured men in metal dress and armour. They did not know how to plough a field or plant a handful of grain. They had knowledge only of fighting.

"One bad harvest and there will be another famine." Mother nodded her head over the dim fire under the cooking pot. She sat down on a stool and began to twist wool into thread with the distaff that was often in her hands.

She looked up at Garth in a way she had never done before. "You are growing quickly," she said. "There are things you are ready to know." She paused and looked down at her work before going on. "Your real father, Garth, came to Dodding in a time of famine." She talked distantly, as though she were suddenly far away. "He staggered to the priest's door and the priest took him in. For days he had eaten only bark from the trees."

Garth was almost frightened to hear more. Mother had never talked this way before about his father. Often he had wondered about the man who many in the village said he resembled. But no one spoke about his father. It was as if there were a secret, a sadness about him, and Garth shied away from asking about him.

"It was like this, Garth," Mother continued. "I remember each word, for I was a servant girl in Sir John's manor house then and I listened to all that went on there. One day your father walked in, tall and proud, with hair as bright as the sun. He had two tools in his hand—a large chisel and a mallet—and he asked to sell them for the right to use a portion of Sir John's land.

"'The tools are worth six shillings, eight pence,' Sir John said.

"Then your father gave him his tools and Sir John gave him a white rod as a sign that he was letting him use some land. Your father knelt and put his hands between Sir John's hands and promised to be true and faithful to him and never leave the manor.

"As for his death, I've always told you the truth, Garth, or part of it. I will speak of this once and then you must ask no more. It grieves me too

much." Mother's voice was low. "Before he came
to Sir John he travelled from place to place as a
carver of stone. He was a free man with a proud
craft. Then one day the fingers of his right hand
were crushed by falling rocks. He could no longer
carve and he could find no work. He sold his freedom to Sir John to stay alive, but the selling of this
freedom is what killed him. His death came when
you were only two . . ."

Mother paused. "He always kept the small
chisel you have in your belt. I've never told you
why he had it because I didn't want you to be un-
happy with your lot. Some people said your father
put on airs because he'd been a free man. I didn't
want you to dream of things *you* couldn't have."

Mother paused again but now she smiled,
"Don't think ill of him, Garth. The week after he
arrived in Dodding, I danced with him at the
Lammas feast. We fell in love. Sir John gave us
permission to marry and we were given this cottage where you were born. He was so proud of
you."

Garth looked at his own strong fingers and
thought of the horror of having them crushed.
His dreams, too, would be destroyed if this hap-
pened to him.

Mother stood to give the soup another stir.
She spoke now as though to herself.

"And we have been blessed, too. Goderic took
us in. He is a good, honest, hard-working man.
With him we have no worry of starvation. For this

I am grateful."

Garth touched the small chisel. Again the disturbing words rang in his ears.

"It's a link with the past and a hope for the future."

❧ 7 ❧

Lammas Sunday came with clear skies and bright sunshine. Garth greeted it with mingled joy and sadness. Edmund would not be sharing it with him and Hawkin would be striding about with his lurking suspicions. He tried not to look at the tools on the wall and the place where the pruning hook should be. Goderic had not missed it yet.

But his spirits lifted when Mother laid out the fresh kirtles, shirts and tunics saved just for the holidays. She even handed both Goderic and Garth fresh broad-brimmed straw hats that she had made as a surprise. They did not wash their faces or hands. This was a privilege enjoyed only by the household of Sir John. Garth yearned for the feel of clean skin and he wondered why no one else among the peasants ever mentioned such a longing.

As usual Goderic, Mother, and Garth plodded one behind the other along the path towards the church. They arrived to find the peasant boys and girls gathering around the yew tree to dance the carol. They were joining hands to form a circle.

Garth paused before he joined them to be sure he would hold the hand of a fair maid instead of one with a wart on her chin or a missing front tooth. He stopped suddenly. The strange spinning in his head came upon him and a vision flashed before his eyes of a young girl with floating raven hair. It was she he wanted to stand beside.

"What a stupid fool I am," Garth muttered. He shook his spinning head and grabbed the hand of Edith, the daughter of their neighbour Wat. He liked her round cheeks and saucy eyes.

Usually it was Edmund who stood apart from the circle to mark time with a little bell, but this year it was Edith's sister. She struck up the ballad of "Harvest Home" and everyone began dancing round and round to her singing.

"Edmund would sing it so much better," Garth whispered to Edith.

All kept time to the rhythm of the music and the words.

> Come, Roger and Nell,
> Come, Simpkin and Bell,
> Each lad with his lass hither come;
> With singing and dancing
> And pleasure advancing,
> To celebrate harvest-home!

The dancing was merry and carefree but it

ended abruptly with the arrival of Sir John and Lady Margaret and their attendants. Garth turned his face to avoid seeing Hawkin when he entered among them.

Walter the priest, with his thin and fragile face, came to the door of the church to bid them enter. Since he was from the village of Dodding and had grown up in the hut of a peasant, he was loved and not feared. He spoke the language of the people. But his office in the parish of St. Peter's was a holy charge to Walter. He spoke, as he understood, from the little learning that had been allowed him.

Some priests, Garth had heard, would order the curse of the church on any who danced and made merry in the churchyard before the service. But Walter the priest always said, "Men may lawfully make mirth on a holiday. God forbid all else."

As they entered the church Garth looked at once at the altar. The small brown Lammas loaf *was* there. It was a sign that the harvest could begin tomorrow. The peasants and nobles of Dodding were assured there would be food for the coming winter.

Walter the priest blessed the loaf, and special prayers were said for the victory of King Edward and Sir John's safe return to Dodding.

The service was brief. Garth hurried out of doors as soon as it ended. On such a day Goderic would not be watching him. He would speed to the hut of Edmund at once before the Lammas meal started and the afternoon dancing and games began.

As Garth approached Edmund's hut he saw a thin spiral of smoke rising above the iron cooking pot. He smiled, for he could smell the fragrance of eel cooking in the soup.

Garth pushed open the sagging door. On a straw mat in the corner, Edmund sat upright, holding his swollen head in his hands.

"Blessed Lammas Day, Edmund," Garth shouted, swinging wide the door.

Edmund lifted his red, puffed face. Behind the pain in his eyes there was a glint of his old good humour.

"Greetings to you, Garth." Garth caught a teasing merriment in Edmund's voice and knew that at heart his friend had not changed.

But his scarred face tore at Garth's heart. He exploded in anger. "May the devil boil Hawkin's body in the blood of turtles and snakes!" he cried, shaking a rotting beam that supported the straw thatch above their heads. Bits and pieces of straw rained down on them. Edmund cupped his aching head in his hands as though to protect himself from more injury.

Garth's fury ended as quickly as it began. He knelt beside his friend.

"I do you more harm than good, Edmund," he said. "But I can bring you food, and when your face is no longer swollen I'll ask Mother to make

you a hat of straw that will cover all signs of that
devilish scar."

Edmund motioned for his friend to draw
near.

"If I don't have to shout at you, Garth, then I
can talk."

Garth settled himself eagerly beside his friend.
Edmund had seen beyond the boundaries of
Dodding! If John the smith was telling the truth,
Edmund had been to the great cathedral of Isle,
for they said he was begging from the monks at
the Priory when they caught him.

"How did you leave the village?" Garth asked
eagerly.

"In a cart filled with hay. It was warm and a
good place to hide until we came to a land called
the Fens. It's a place of muck and swamps, Garth,
that bubbles from inside the earth." Edmund's
small, usually merry eyes narrowed with fear.

"It was night and the black closed around us.
The spirits were crying and piping. Then our cart
lost the road." Here he stopped, for the memory
set him shuddering.

"The muck and the mire oozed against us,
Garth. You would have thought we were riding
through a kettle of soup."

"The cart must have jerked," Garth said. "It's a
wonder you didn't fly straight out of the straw."

"I almost did." Edmund tried to smile. He
paused and his eyes shifted from merriment to a
strange, excited glow.

"Someday you must see the cathedral of Isle, Garth. It is greater than St. Peter's, greater than Sir John's manor house. It could hold all of the forest of Dodding inside its nave!"

Edmund looked about and then lowered his voice until it was less than a whisper. "I'm going to run away again, Garth, and live near the cathedral. There is a choir for young boys and I dream of singing with them. I will let my hair grow long in front to cover the scar. Father will miss me, but it will be one less mouth for him to feed."

Garth grabbed his friend's shoulders, but before he could speak, both boys heard cries from the village green. The Lammas meal was starting and soon the games would begin.

"You must go, Garth." Edmund lay back on the straw. "Bring me food and tell me about the games. Now hurry."

Garth squeezed his friend's limp hand. He drew the mantle over him, for he seemed to have fallen asleep.

Garth ran through the common fields and back to the village green. He hadn't thought once of Goderic's pruning hook.

❦ 8 ❦

At the village green Garth found tottering boards already set upon trestles for tables. Friends and neighbours were seated around them. Garth searched for a place to sit.

Joints of tough old mutton sizzled on the turning spits nearby. Wooden bowls steamed with thick soup and wooden mugs were brimming with ale. Even the loaves of bread were plentiful and anyone could cut with his own knife a slab of meat from the cooked joints. Garth remembered eating meat from joints at the Christmas feast but he hadn't tasted any since.

Thomas the stone carver strode by, stopping beside Garth. "For someone who works as hard as you," he laughed, "I have an extra piece of cheese." He leaned closer and whispered, "And here's another for Edmund."

Garth thanked the stone carver warmly. He stuffed Edmund's piece into a shabby purse which hung from his girdle. When no one was looking he added chunks of bread and bits of meat. He knew that Edmund would be denied the Lammas meal as part of his punishment.

Garth also knew that on a day such as this no one would be watching him, not even Goderic. They all would be groggy with feasting and ale.

Soon the lively tunes of bagpipes could be heard rippling through the yellow leaves of the white-stemmed birches that grew beside the ancient yew in the churchyard. The young people raced from the feasting tables to hear them.

Garth's excitement and joy swept away his troubles of the past few days. His feet beat a rhythm in the soft grass and he made a point of standing beside Edith.

The minstrel put down his bagpipes and reached for a fiddle that was slung over his back. In a deep voice he sang:

> Come, gentlemen all and listen awhile
> And a story to you I'll unfold.
> I'll tell you how Robin Hood received
> the bishop
> When he robbed him of his gold.

The peasants of Dodding gathered around, laughing and shouting. They knew the ballad from beginning to end and never tired of hearing all the verses.

Garth had only one regret—that Edmund could not be with him, though he might be listening in his hut. He knew that his friend dreamed of singing and acting and perhaps becoming a minstrel, just as he dreamed of becoming a carver of stone.

Thomas the carver was singing with a group nearby. He joined Garth for a moment and bent to whisper in his ear.

"I've heard of your good tending of Edmund. I've sent a potion of herbs with Egbert to hasten his healing and I've also sent him some food."

Garth smiled warmly at the carver.

"It's good to end my stay in Dodding with feasting and singing," Thomas answered his smile.

"End your stay!" Garth stood rigid among the swaying singers.

"I return to Isle tomorrow," Thomas said rather wistfully.

A line of dancers jogged through the crowd, catching Thomas by the hand and swinging him off through the meadows.

Inside Garth a burning candle lost its flame. Just knowing Thomas had somehow given him hope that someday he too might be a carver of stone. Instinctively Garth fingered the chisel at his waist.

Then someone called for the game "Hot Cockle Hot," the boys and girls swept Garth into their circle, and for a moment he forgot about Thomas.

Edith whipped a kerchief from her head to blindfold him. Players began striking his hands.

"It's Walter," Garth called half-heartedly.

"Nay, nay," came the answer.

Then a small hand struck ever so lightly.

"It's Edith," Garth guessed at once, but for some reason he found himself wishing it had been the girl with the flowing black hair.

"My brain is addled," he cried and tore off the blindfold.

Edith had not heard. There was too much boisterous laughter around them. Garth no longer wanted to play. It was time for the boys and girls to pair off and stroll together as far as the waste. They must return by sundown.

"Would you go for a stroll with me, Edith?" Garth asked. "We will stop to see Edmund."

"Aye," replied Edith eagerly, "but first I must tell my family." She hurried away.

There was a sudden hush among the merrymakers. Sir John and his family were riding by.

Garth found himself close enough to them to touch the toe of Sir John's boot, until his daughter Agnes drove her horse between them. For one instant her eyes met Garth's.

"Oh!" she cried. "There's the boy who tried to steal fish from the river."

Steward Hawkin, riding behind, jerked his horse towards Garth as though drawn by an archer's bow.

"He has not yet been punished for this sin." His words seemed to curl like smoke from his thin lips. "I will deal with him tomorrow."

Garth shuddered. Sir John had not heard. He was speaking to the gathering crowds of people about another matter.

"We have been blessed with victory in war and today we are blessed with a harvest that will soon be abundant." He lifted his strong, steady voice. "We must show gratitude with an offering to the Priory of Isle."

The people nodded in assent. Sir John continued, "Early tomorrow morning we are sending two carts filled with sheaves of grain to Isle."

The joy of Lammas drained from Garth's heart. He was going to be punished after all, and Thomas was leaving. Then, as he listened to Sir John, a spark of hope rekindled the flame within him. He recalled that Edmund had escaped in a cart of hay.

By the time Edith joined Garth he was in no mood for a stroll. He must talk with Edmund at once. He grabbed Edith's hand and hurried her to the swineherd's hut.

They found Edmund sitting huddled beneath the sprawling apple boughs that were as misshapen as the tree's twisted trunk. A tattered straw hat covered his head and from its many holes sprouted tufts of stiff brown hair. He lifted his hand as a greeting, but his head remained down.

"Ye poor lad," Edith cried with a rush of pity and motherliness. She knelt beside Edmund and looked into his swollen face. The sight was a shock, but she didn't recoil. Instead, she gently ministered to the injured boy. Edmund could use such care now, Garth thought gratefully.

In no time Edith discovered the filth inside the hut and declared it would take every minute of the ebbing daylight to put it in order. Garth was relieved. If she busied herself inside, he could talk with Edmund undisturbed.

Garth sat down beside his friend and at once a steady stream of words poured from his mouth. His burdens had become too great to hold inside. He told of the punishment that might come in the morning, the ominous words of Hawkin, the departure of Thomas—and finally the two carts and their sheaves of grain.

Edmund's body tensed. His hand tightened around his friend's wrist. His lips pressed against Garth's ear and he whispered, "We must escape in the carts—you in one, I in the other. It is our only chance for a life that is better."

Garth gasped now that the idea of escape was out in the open. Did he have the courage to say yes to this desperate and dangerous venture?

"I'll take Edith back at once," he answered. "I'll come back and meet you here. We must talk more."

As he rose to go, Garth saw the pruning hook lying behind Edmund in the bramble and the weeds, and realized he had forgotten it yet again. He bent low beside Edmund and said, "Goderic's pruning hook is on the ground beside you. Guard it well until I return."

Garth raced back with Edith to the laughing villagers. She was drawn at once into another circle of dancers. Garth drifted away into the shadows.

He watched the crowd and saw even dour Goderic laughing. Of all nights of the year, Garth thought, this was the best to make plans that were secret. Even Mother was lost to his whereabouts as she huddled with the women in merry laughter and talk.

Just as Garth turned to leave, a young friend, William, sidled up to him. His black eyes were narrowed and he leaned forward like a dog sniffing prey. He had the makings of a spy, Garth thought.

"I heard about the ox-carts going to Isle," he said. "Sir John is sending his youngest knight, Sir Robert, and his squire to guard against robbers and cutthroats, and Thomas the carver is going. Even Wat will travel with them to drive and tend the oxen."

"You have heard much," Garth replied easily, not wanting to show too much concern or interest. "But who cares about that when there is feasting and celebrating all about us?"

William couldn't be stopped. "They are loading the carts now and will leave at daybreak. Sir John himself will see them off."

"You should be there too." Garth patted young William on the back and strode away. The news he had told him was priceless.

Garth looked back at the villagers. The thought of leaving his mother suddenly tore at his heart, even though he knew she was secure with Goderic. She had said as much. And whatever fears she might have for him, she had given him his father's chisel—and he knew what that meant.

"It's a link with the past and a hope for the future." The words resounded again in his head. Any future for him could not be as a peasant in Dodding.

Without warning the tall figure of Hawkin appeared, striding by, his eyes darting left and right as if he were checking on the peasants. His thin mouth seemed to purse with displeasure at the merriment about him. Knowing what might await him in the morning, Garth trembled in spite of his anger with the steward, and moved farther back into the shadows. He saw Thomas nearby, but he was talking intimately with Walter the priest. Watching him, Garth realized that Dodding would be a hard place to live in without Thomas. And if Edmund was going to try to escape again, he would also lose his best friend.

Garth knew that his own decision to run away was settled. He would join Edmund tonight in one of the ox-carts. Now there was no time to waste. He must see Edmund at once. He ran home to his hut. Inside he found the mantle that Mother had retrieved from Edmund. He quickly threw his wooden clogs, his leggings, and his shirt of thick serge into it and made a bundle. His best tunic was the one on his back. He decided to give Edmund most of the food he had taken from the Lammas meal and keep the rest in the purse around his waist. It would be easy to reach from his hiding place in the cart.

But what message of affection could he leave for Mother? Garth reached inside the pocket of his tunic and found a small stone fish that he had chiselled one day in secret. He put it on the straw mat where Mother slept.

It was time to meet Edmund now, for the sun was setting. Garth crept quietly from the hut and hurried down the narrow path.

He found Edmund waiting in front of the swineherd's hut. He, too, had a bundle beside him and an even more tattered purse around his waist. It appeared to be filled with food. Evidently Thomas had sent a whole feast to Edmund from the Lammas meal.

Edmund smiled at Garth, lifting his head, which was swathed in a wrapping of ragged cloth. "I knew you would come. We must go tonight, Garth, together."

Garth whispered at once the news he had heard from William. Edmund nodded. "I have been watching from the top of our hut, and I could see and hear the talk at the loading place. The sheaves of grain and the hay have already been loaded. No one is there now. They have gone to get the pairs of oxen that will be attached to the carts. . . . We must crawl inside the hay now, Garth, before anyone returns."

Garth's heart beat so loudly he wondered if it could be heard as far away as the village green.

Edmund stood and held the pruning hook. "It will help us push a hole inside the hay where we can crawl. And when we cross the devilish Fen country with its swamps and bogs, we'll be glad for it."

"What about Egbert?" Garth asked as they hurried towards the loaded carts.

"He is like Goderic," Edmund whispered. "I have broken the rules of the manor of Dodding with my escape and he will not speak to me. I am only a burden to him now."

Both boys crept slowly towards the carts. The evening dusk was on their side and a cloud blessedly covered the full harvest moon.

Garth took the pruning hook and pushed holes into the hay in both carts.

"Before we crawl inside," Edmund whispered breathlessly, "I must tell you what I heard. The carts will leave before early morning mass. A pilgrim is also going along with Sir Robert and

Thomas the carver. It seems he knows the holes to avoid on the winding road and the dangers of the causeway through the swamps of the Fens."

Edmund offered more caution. "When you see the water bubble from inside the earth, Garth, you will know that we have come to the Fens. The crying and piping of the spirits will chill your blood. But they will never find us, buried in all this hay.

"And," he added quickly, "if we fall into a bog, we will need something that will hold to a tree limb. The pruning hook will do this. We can't swim like the breeding folk in the Fens. They are like fish, living in water over their necks most of their days."

Garth flung this worry from his thoughts. He'd been in water up to his neck when he fished in the lord's river and he liked the feel of it. But to have his head go under the water was another matter. He would keep the pruning hook.

Someday when he was a free man, he thought, after he had lived safely away from Dodding for a year and a day, he would send the tool to Goderic. He would shine and polish it until it looked better than when he took it.

Garth shuddered. He lifted Edmund into the largest cart, and they clasped hands for an instant. "We must pray to the God above to protect and guide us, Edmund," Garth said. "And we must have a way to call to one another along the way."

"I know," said Edmund. "We will whistle—

high for danger, low for all clear."

"Of course," Garth answered as he helped his small friend with his bundle inside the hay. He covered him carefully so he could not be seen.

Garth heard the ox-teams approaching. He quickly jumped into his cart, holding both his bundle and the pruning hook. Then he used the curved hook to pull the hay around him.

Garth whistled softly to his friend.

Another whistle was his reassuring answer.

🐚 10 🐚

The warmth of the hay and his own exhaustion put Garth to sleep. He didn't waken until his head banged against the wooden handle of his pruning hook. He tried to jump up but he couldn't move. On all sides of him were the prickly stems of drying hay. His body jogged from side to side. Then a strange voice droned into his ears.

"My friends," the voice said, "we are on our way to the great cathedral of Isle."

"Isle!" Garth remembered. He had fallen asleep. He was in the cart of hay escaping to Isle. It was daylight! No one had discovered him yet. But what about Edmund? He couldn't risk whistling to him now.

Garth turned slowly onto his stomach. In this position he could see through a small opening in the hay. The voice, he discovered, came from a plump little pilgrim wrapped in a black serge cloak. He rode with ease on the back of an ambling mule. His wide hat, bearing the badges of shrines that he had visited, bobbed up and down.

Thomas the carver, tall and straight, jogged along beside him on his horse.

Another voice, loud and commanding, broke the pilgrim's steady drone. "We must go slowly now. There are dangerous holes in our path."

This voice, Garth saw, belonged to Sir Robert, who was followed by a young squire. Garth was surprised that Sir Robert was not wearing his full armour. Perhaps for this pilgrimage of thanksgiving he had left many of his war garments at home. However, his gilded spurs, which displayed his rank, were in place.

The cart stopped abruptly, swaying from side to side as though the earth beneath it were in motion. Garth almost worried that he would be spilled onto the ground.

He could hear Wat, who walked ahead leading the oxen, shout in anger, "Who could have dug a hole to get clay in the middle of this road? Whoever he is, a whipping would be good for him."

Garth twisted in the hay, drawing his legs under his stomach, to make himself as small as possible. He looked again through the hay. This time he saw Sir Robert riding his horse around a cavity almost as big as the mill pond in Dodding.

"We must travel around this hole," Sir Robert said, directing his squire to place logs in front of it as a warning.

Garth had not seen the young squire before and decided he must be a new boy who had come to Sir John's manor to train for the knighthood. He had a stiff face that was pale and thin and he twisted and turned on his pony with the weight of a long leather scabbard that hung diagonally across his back. The hilt appeared behind his left shoulder. He carried the sword for Sir Robert, who would buckle it around his waist when he dismounted.

Garth could see Wat sitting on the dusty road for a moment's rest. He was rubbing his tired legs. Garth knew that he had walked since daybreak while the others rested their limbs on the backs of their beasts.

Garth himself longed to stand and stretch his legs. He was hungry too and his mouth was dry, but he would have to wait for all of this until darkness came and those about him had fallen asleep.

If only he could talk with Edmund and know that he was safe. This would also have to wait until dark.

The pilgrim began to speak again. "The great waterways of the Fens," he said, sweeping his arms before him, "are one with those of the North Sea. Ships cross the wide sea up the Fenland waters to Isle. They are loaded with rich jewelled relics, spices and incense, and sacred books for our cathedral."

The talking stopped abruptly, for grey clouds were beginning to sweep across the sky. In their wake came a strong, chill wind with sprays of rain. The pilgrim hunched into his cloak, pulling a cowl over his head. Sir Robert and his squire and Thomas rode erect, ignoring the rain. Garth could not catch a view of Wat, but he knew he must be miserable, plodding through the cold splashing puddles with his bare feet. Garth could hear the second cart rattling behind him. It was a comfort just to know that Edmund was nearby.

The wind turned into a gale. It whistled as it swirled around the carts, ripping loose great strands of hay until Garth feared he might be uncovered.

"There is an inn, the White Swan, not far up this road," Garth heard the pilgrim call to Sir Robert. "Perhaps we should stop to dry our bones and quench our thirst."

"That we'll do," Sir Robert shouted back to him.

A swinging board, banging and rattling in the wind, soon came into view. Through the sweeps of rain, Garth could see a white swan painted on it. The carts creaked to a stop beneath the overhanging thatch of the White Swan Inn. Cracks about its door revealed streaks of flickering light, a sure sign that a warm fire burned inside.

At once everyone abandoned the carts and hurried inside. Even Wat, who should have stayed by the oxen, joined the others. Garth heard him mutter, "No thief will be out in a storm such as this."

As Wat closed the inn door behind him, Garth realized that he was free to call to Edmund; there was no need to use their signal.

"Edmund!" "Garth!" The calls and answers came almost at once.

"I have been sleeping through most of the journey, Garth"—Edmund sounded almost gleeful—"and my head is not so full of pain. . . . The hay is soft and smells cleaner than my mat at home. Let's crawl outside, Garth, and stretch our legs."

"No, no, Edmund!" Garth called. "I can see Wat coming from the inn to check on the oxen."

There was instant silence between them.

Garth could hear Wat sloshing about in the wind and rain. The carts began to move and soon the wind died down. They were being sent to a shelter provided by the inn. Little did Wat know, Garth thought, that he was keeping two runaway peasant boys dry as well as protecting the oxen.

As soon as they were alone Garth called to Edmund. "We must not crawl outside, Edmund. The oxen would be disturbed."

"Aye," Edmund answered at once, "but we can eat some food and talk with one another."

The two boys chatted back and forth until the fires went out inside the inn. After a while they slept briefly until they were wakened by Sir Robert shouting.

"We must start at once before the storm gains more fury."

Garth knew that they were nearing the causeway, a road over grounds of such a treacherous nature that it had to be built up and strengthened with stonework and timber.

It was impossible for Garth or Edmund to watch their party assemble. The dark, stormy skies were like a blindfold. But in a short time the carts started to jog again and the little pilgrim began his talking.

"Take heed, my friends." He had to shout to be heard above the wind. "If you lick your lips and the moisture has the taste of salt, the Great Sea has come raging in at high tide over the Fens."

The winds whipped into greater fury and the sky became a billowy canopy of shifting clouds. Rocking and swaying, the lumbering cart wheels hit some stones and Garth looked down onto a bridge. It arched above a foaming river.

"'Tis the River Ouse," he heard the pilgrim cry. "Most times it runs a placid course and barely seems to move."

Garth looked through the hay and saw a barge on the flooding river. Even in the dim light he could make out its load of stones and logs. He wondered if the stones might be building materials for the great cathedral of Isle. Water fowl flapped about everywhere and wild gcose flew, disturbed and restless, in the sedgy fields.

Thicker patches of mist and fog rose and fell and the carts slowed almost to a stop. There seemed to be neither ditch nor hedge to act as guides along the causeway now. One wrong turn, it seemed to Garth, and they could plunge into the water.

The drowsy scene of fog and rain, the slow jog of the cart, the warmth of his covering mantle under the hay lulled Garth to sleep, in spite of his fierce pledge to be constantly alert to danger.

When he woke, the view through his hole in the hay was black. Either night had come or heavy clouds had smothered the sun. The jogging wheels of the cart were still and an angry, roaring sound was drawing closer and closer.

"Is it the roar of the Great Sea?" Garth wondered.

The sea! Garth stiffened with terror. He forced himself to lick the moisture around his lips. It tasted of salt! The high tide of the sea had broken the banks that held it back. Sea water was washing over the flat, marshy fens.

Garth grasped his pruning hook. The oxen were stamping and neighing. He tunnelled his way through the hay. There was no need for him to hide any longer. The wind tore against the cart with pounding fury. Hay and sheaves of grain flew in all directions. But where was the knight, his squire, the pilgrim, poor Wat, Thomas? The small plot of ground around him was empty and Edmund's cart had disappeared from sight!

Garth set the oxen loose. They could at least swim if they had no carts to pull. Then he drew his mantle tightly about him, grabbed his bundle in one hand and the pruning hook in the other, and felt with his feet the path of the causeway. Icy water now swirled up to his knees.

Perhaps, Garth thought, if he made his way slowly along the solid turf of the causeway, he would come to Isle. As he pushed ahead he believed that he was indeed seeing devils flying with the winds of the storm as Edmund had predicted. If only Edmund were with him. He shouted his name, but the roaring storm swallowed every word. A flock of sheep floated by, leaderless and dazed. Great sheaves of floating grain bumped back and forth among them. Garth could do nothing but walk firmly on the causeway and let them pass.

The water about his legs rose higher. The taste of salt was strong, and it took all his strength just to remain upright against the force of the onrushing current.

Step by step Garth plodded ahead, looking constantly for some signal that might indicate a town or people nearby.

Then, finally, there *was* a signal. A distant fire was sending sprays of orange and blue light into the sky.

Punting boats began to appear, heading towards the flames. The causeway that Garth was following, lit by the distant fire, seemed to lead directly towards them. Fiery arms appeared to reach out to welcome him. At last he stumbled into a circle of men, women, and children huddled around the warmth. They moved aside to give him a place. A brown jug of ale was being passed among them.

"Are you a stranger here?" someone asked.

Garth nodded, then drank from the jug and passed it along. He quickly scanned each face, hoping that one of them might be Edmund or Thomas. But all of them were also strangers to him.

Another punt arrived, landing near the fire.

Garth looked up. The wet and tattered "strangers" were Sir Robert and his youthful squire! Garth hid his face beneath his mantle. He grabbed his bundle and his pruning hook and ran into a forest of alders outside the ring of heat and light.

🐚 **11** 🐚

Garth felt his way slowly over the sea-washed land. A yearning for the fire behind him grew as strongly as the pains of hunger in his stomach. But the thought of Sir Robert's haggard face was enough to drive him on.

The dark began to lift and a light from another fire appeared. Farther down the shoreline was another blaze, and then another. They were rescue fires for the many Fenland people caught in the storm, Garth realized. He crawled towards the blaze nearest him and scanned every face. But they were strangers—straggly, thin, and gloomy.

One man held out a flask for Garth to drink from. Another offered him bread to eat. And still another moved aside to give him room before the flames. He felt a warmth inside him for their kindly manner.

Garth sank exhausted to the ground. The crackling flames held back the dark and wet and cold and warmed his body. He placed his bundle before him, feeling at the top to be certain his chisel was there. He sat on the pruning hook. The

Fenland people drew tighter together about him and he shut his eyes and slept.

The dawn that came was grey and sunless. But the blowing wind held no rain and the foaming salt water seemed to be seeping back towards the sea.

Garth woke and sat upright. A face just opposite in the circle of flame was one he knew. He jumped to his feet. It was the black-cloaked pilgrim who had ridden beside his cart. The little man talked to those around him and gave Garth only a moment's glance.

"Of course, he doesn't know me." Garth sank to the ground again. He had watched the pilgrim from his crack through the hay. The pilgrim no doubt thought him just another boy from the Fens.

Garth leaned towards him to hear what he might be saying. Perhaps he would talk of Edmund, Thomas, or Wat.

"My good mule was washed from under me and my companions went in all directions," he was telling anyone who would listen.

The Fenland folk around him had cares and troubles of their own. They paid no attention to him. In all the crowd, there was only one attentive, listening face, and that was Garth's. The pilgrim noticed this and grabbed Garth's sleeve and drew him to his side.

"No doubt you've lost the good folks that you came along to serve." He had scanned Garth's rough and muddied tunic and guessed that he was a villein—a peasant.

Garth only nodded, being fearful to speak before someone who had come from Dodding so recently.

"You must come with me, my boy, and aid me with my needs. I must yet make my pilgrimage to the great cathedral of Isle."

He handed Garth his staff and bundle and puffed, as fat men do, when struggling to his feet.

"You are a sturdy boy and bright." He looked up, for Garth was taller than he. His eyes narrowed shrewdly when he saw the pruning hook, but he said nothing about it.

The pilgrim showed no sign of recognition and Garth deemed it good fortune to find someone who knew the way—and someone, too, who told such tales as he had never heard before.

The pious man muttered to himself, and Garth caught only snatches of his chatter. "We must find the Monk's Causeway . . . then cross the Great Bridge . . . I shall have coins for the Bridge Reeve."

The pilgrim did not ask Garth's name nor pry into his past. Garth had to stop himself from asking the whereabouts of Edmund and Thomas. The thought that they might have drowned weighed on him heavily.

The morning brightened as the hidden sun pressed against the clouds. Murky forms emerged. Lakes and marshes, which the night before had been a raging sea, took shape again. Here and there the tips of reeds pushed their way above the water and great flat barges laden with slender shafts of grey-brown marble poled along a canal.

"It's marble from the quarries in Dorset," the pilgrim said, noticing Garth's eager interest. "And see those eight teams of oxen beyond the bridge? It will take all of those beasts harnessed to a sledge to pull the heavy marble to the great cathedral."

Garth and the pilgrim were soon joined by others travelling to Isle. Some had been hurt in the storm, like the man limping barefoot by Garth's side.

A knight on horseback appeared. He was clothed in armour as though he had just come from battle. His squire rode close beside him. Garth peered swiftly at their faces, afraid they might be Sir Robert and his thin-faced squire. But they were strangers. A sick man lying upon a litter carried by his friends was hurried past. He was knotted up with swollen joints.

Suddenly a bagpipe broke into a joyful, shrill tune. Garth wheeled about and saw a troupe made up of a minstrel, a juggler, and an acrobat.

All of them crossed the bridge together. At the end of it, each one was stopped by a reeve, who demanded a toll. The pilgrim handed him some pennies for himself and Garth. Others gave a catch of fish or eel instead of coins. Garth felt good to be walking side by side with all these people, not caring at the moment if one were knight,

priest, peasant, or lady. It would be a happy cara-
van, he thought, if only Edmund and Thomas
were among them.

Garth kept close beside the pilgrim, who continued to load him down with more and more
bundles.

The sights on either side of them fascinated
Garth. They passed granaries and warehouses,
doors open to receive the goods unloading from
ships and barges. Up ahead, a town like nothing
Garth had ever seen loomed before them. As they
entered Isle the path beneath their feet changed
from mud to cobblestones. Garth's bare feet wob-
bled over them and he quickly pulled his clogs
from his bundle and put them on. The horses'
hooves clattered as they walked and the wagon
wheels passing by them clanged over the stones.
Cries of pedlars rose shrilly over the din. "Fresh
fish! Hot sheep's feet! Rushes green, rushes—oh!"

Garth was excited by all the new sights and
would have run in every direction, but the wary
pilgrim caught him by the cord around his tunic
and held him tight.

They came to narrow streets that wound between crowded houses. Some were built of stone,
Garth noticed, and others of rough plaster held
together by huge oak beams with thatching for a
roof.

Garth couldn't believe that the houses went
up three and four storeys, jutting out over the
street like towering cliffs. He slipped suddenly on

a puddle of fish skins and scales that had been dumped from a bucket high above his head.

The pilgrim walked now along lesser lanes. Some were filled with cats and dogs and puddles of mud. On one was a swinging sign with a painted shoe.

"Only shoemakers live along this street," the pilgrim explained, for there were others in the group besides Garth who had never set foot in a town.

The next lane needed no sign: the fish smell was enough, as were the fragrant smells from the bakers' lane. Those with coins bought bread. Garth feared he might go hungry, but the pilgrim handed him a generous half-loaf.

The town seemed to spin before Garth in a mixture of awe, excitement, bewilderment, and surprise. How could he make sense of it all?

Then he looked up. High above the town and surrounded by a wall of stone rose the majestic towers and spires of Isle Cathedral. They were dim behind some fog, but Garth instantly felt the power of their sweeping presence. The pilgrim stopped abruptly as though transfixed.

"The cathedral is the heart and soul of Isle," he said with feeling.

Suddenly the cathedral's mighty bells began to ring and all other noises ceased. Garth hardly dared to move. He looked up again but the spires were gone, erased from the sky by a thick, dark fog.

Suddenly out of this darkness rode two horse-men of knightly bearing. Garth looked into their faces and shuddered. It was Sir Robert and his youthful squire.

The pilgrim grasped his shoulder, leaning heavily upon him. He couldn't run.

🐚 12 🐚

Garth knew that he must hide. Sir Robert would recognize him in an instant. They had met one day in Dodding at John's smithy. Sir Robert had caught him carving a devil's face of Hawkin in wood. He had whipped him on the spot and crushed the carving with his foot.

The men drew near. Garth realized that even if he could break free of the pilgrim's hold on him, he could never outrun a knight and squire on horseback. He felt as though a snake were slithering towards him and he was doing nothing but waiting for it to strike.

Perhaps, though, he had one chance. He dropped his bundles and the pruning hook and drew the hood of his mantle over his head.

"An aching tooth," he mumbled, bending low to gather up his goods and pull the mud-streaked hood more tightly around his head.

The pilgrim gave him scant attention. He greeted Sir Robert jovially and urged him to join their party. They talked about the flood and how each one had managed to be rescued and finally pulled ashore. Garth almost raised his head when he heard them say that Wat was missing and both of the carts had floated away. They did not mention Thomas or the cart that Edmund was in. At least they did not say they had drowned, Garth thought with little comfort.

"What waif have you beside you?" Sir Robert's voice held scorn.

"A sturdy villein washed up from the sea who aids me with my load." The pilgrim reached again for Garth's hunched shoulder. "He's doubled up with pain from an aching tooth, poor lad."

Sir Robert seemed to have little further interest in Garth and turned his horse to trot beside a travelling coach drawn by four horses carrying an elegant lady. They appeared to know each other. Garth heard the lady greet Sir Robert and then say thinly, with a mouth that puckered as though drawn together with a thread, "These inhabitants of Isle have a turfy scent and fenny posture, Sir Robert."

Whatever did she mean? Garth wondered. To him, some of the people smelled of fish and some of bread. The sights and sounds did not displease his nose or eyes, even though it was difficult to see from inside his hood.

Grey clouds scudded above the muddy windswept land that held the cathedral of Isle, although the cathedral still could not be seen. At times it was a strain just to see ahead or gauge a turn that might be coming in the narrow streets.

The pilgrim huffed and wheezed. Although Garth helped to bear him along, his shoulder was no substitute for the drowned mule that had carried the small, fat man across the causeway.

At one point Garth dropped his pruning hook and had to stop the party to rescue it.

"It's strange," Garth heard the young squire say to Sir Robert, "that a poor villein carries such a tool. Could it be his?"

Garth knew it was dangerous to attract attention. He felt inside the folds of his tunic where his chisel was now securely fastened. If they saw this other tool, they would surely brand him a thief.

At a left turn in the street ahead, Garth saw a great line of solemn people. They tugged and strained together as they pulled a thick rope. It was attached to a slow-moving cart piled high with heavy stones.

Stones for the great cathedral! They were at last coming near it, Garth realized.

At that moment a patch of sun broke through the clouds. It revealed in one stroke a scene of such awe-inspiring beauty that the travellers all stopped and gazed upward. It was as though they had been struck with a shimmering sword of lightning. Beyond the houses of the narrow street, on a small green hill, stood the massive, towering cathedral of Isle.

Garth's hood fell back and off his face. He neither cared nor thought who might be looking for him at this moment. He was trying to draw on some familiar sight within his past that could compare with what he saw.

Then he felt the strange buzzing in his head that had come so often in Dodding. He closed his eyes to wait for it to fade, and in his mind's eye there appeared a small picture of the cathedral he was seeing now. He opened his eyes and it disappeared. He looked again at the real scene before him.

The cathedral loomed above him, like a great grey ship pointing its towers and turrets to the sky, riding a wave in an endless flat landscape. Was it a miracle from God—a great stone ark, holding onto heaven with its upward spires? The town around its base, moated on all sides by reed beds, lakes, and marshes, grew smaller as Garth looked at the cathedral towers.

He hoped no one would speak. This moment was too precious. But the pilgrim could not be silenced.

"The ground you walk upon is holy," he proclaimed, stopping all those around him in the cobblestone market square by the cathedral's northeast wall, where there were small booths displaying fish and clothes and trinkets for sale.

The pilgrim's voice rose to a high pitch, for now he was competing with the noise of merchants and cart wheels, as well as the ringing sound of chisel on stone from the nearby stone masons' yard.

"The building of this cathedral," he cried,

"goes back hundreds of years and it still goes on."

The numbers and time meant little to Garth. The group moved towards the stone yard. Garth was fascinated by what he saw. The long procession of men dragging the heavy stones was moving towards it. The ring of pounding mallets and chisels set a rhythm to the steps of those walking close by.

Piles of stones filled the yard beside the cathedral's northeast side. Scurrying about between them were busy stone masons, their grey tunics and hose powdered with stone dust. Even their faces were white with the dust, Garth noticed. Their leather aprons had the cast of grey stone. These were the stone carvers for the cathedral of Isle! Garth's heart beat wildly. This was where Thomas would surely be found!

Two men hammered iron wedges along the side of a large stone, splitting it apart. One man sat upon a flat stone, chiselling a delicate pattern of leaves and intertwining stems upon a small stone held between his knees.

Garth could have gone on watching forever, but suddenly he heard the loud voice of Sir Robert's squire behind him.

"The tall boy with the yellow hair who helps our pilgrim looks like one of the villeins from Dodding," he said.

"Of course! That's where I've seen him," said Sir Robert. "And the pruning hook he carries is like those used by the Dodding villeins."

Garth had forgotten to pull his hood back over his head. For a moment he thought his legs were frozen and wouldn't move. The beating of his heart pounded in his ears. He wondered when Sir Robert would pounce upon him.

Garth turned swiftly. Sir Robert was still astride his horse and his squire stood waiting for an order.

"I've not been caught yet," Garth muttered.

A jutting stone before him concealed a small crevice. Garth shook himself free of the pilgrim's hold and, bending down quickly, slid his bundle and the pruning hook into the opening. He dropped the pilgrim's staff and bundle to the ground. With a quick jump he hurdled the stone and raced among the busy masons.

"A runaway! A runaway!" he heard Sir Robert shout.

Garth saw a wooden building in front of him and rushed inside. It was filled with masons' tools, piles of unfinished stones, and a table along one side.

A narrow staircase led upward to a loft. Garth bounded for it, and climbing up with both hands and feet found himself in a dark, low-ceilinged room with pallets rolled up on the floor. It was a place for many men to sleep. Garth crawled to the darkest corner, pulled a pallet in front of him, and covered himself with his mantle.

Below, he heard the rush and hurry of running men. They circled the building and shouted at the stone masons.

"I think he is still running among the stones," Garth heard one mason say when questioned by Sir Robert.

"He cannot be inside the stone masons' lodge. It is forbidden," said another.

Garth lifted his mantle and looked about. He was hiding in the masons' lodge! This was where the workers who carved stones ate and slept and kept their tools. He was so excited that for a second he forgot his fears. If he were a carver of stone he could live in such a building, with space and sturdy beams and new thatching for a roof.

🐚 13 🐚

Outside the lodge, the search for the runaway ended, at least for the moment. Peeking out a small window, Garth saw Sir Robert slowly mount his horse and speak to his squire. No doubt he was telling him to keep a watch for the escaped villein from Dodding. The pilgrim was propped against an uncut stone. He seemed to be sleeping soundly, his round chin tucked into the folds of flesh about his neck.

Garth could not escape now from the lodge. He must stay where he was until both the squire and Sir Robert grew weary of their search. He fixed his attention on the busy stone workers in the yard below, hoping with all his heart that Thomas, and maybe Edmund, would appear among them. If Thomas had drowned, Sir Robert would surely have mentioned it.

As Garth watched the scene below, he noticed a flurry of excitement among the workers in the yard. A tall, stately man was striding towards them from the cathedral. He walked with swinging steps, talking and gesturing, then scanning the

high towers of the cathedral and finally stopping
to chat with several of the stone masons.

The man wore the clothes of a mason, although of sturdier cloth than those about him.
His grey tunic was unstained and his hose were of
the finest leather. A blue cap covered only the top
of the brown hair that hung below his ears. He
carried a T-square under one arm, and as he
walked a lead plummet hanging from his waist
swung to and fro. Garth saw his face when he
stopped beneath him. It was weathered and wrinkled, yet fresh and strong. He placed his hand
upon the shoulder of a young stone carver and
ran his strong fingers over the man's carving,
which Garth could see was a delicate row of leaves.

"Master Mason John," Garth heard someone
call out to him. Garth looked at him with awe.
Here was the man who was the head of all the
stone masons for the great cathedral.

Garth was growing tired of cowering in the
dark corners of the building, and since no one
seemed to be coming inside he began crawling
about the loft. At one spot he stumbled onto a
bundle of wool cloth beneath his feet. He shook it
loose and found it was a worn grey tunic caked
with stone dust. There was also a hood attached to
it, faded but still of sturdy texture. Garth lost no
time in pulling his muddy tunic from his back and
putting on the grey one in its place. The hood was
large and covered all his hair. Who would know
him now? He started to creep towards the stairs

when the door below swung open and labourers from the yard began to enter.

Garth scrambled back into his corner and pulled his mantle and the grey tunic close about him. He stuffed his own clothes far into the darkest corner. Hearty laughter came from the room below, and then the clink of mugs as ale was poured. Shortly, one by one, the men began to climb the stairs and find their pallets in the loft. Garth had a moment of terror fearing that he might be noticed. But there were dozens of men, and they seemed too exhausted to look about in corners. They flung themselves on the straw pallets and most of them were soon asleep.

Nearest Garth, a bent old man shared his pallet with a younger fellow who Garth decided must be new to Isle and unfamiliar with its ways.

The old man began giving him instructions.

"The working hours are good here," he said. "Our breakfast lasts as long as it takes a man to walk a mile. For dinner, we have an hour and a half. And, in the heat of afternoon, there is time for ale and a brief rest."

"And what about the pay?" the young man asked.

"Higher than in most cathedrals or castles where I've worked." The old man lowered his voice, for the work-tired men around him were disgruntled by his talking. "Five pence a day we get in summer, three pence in winter when the days are shorter, and four in spring or autumn—

and Master Mason John pays us promptly by the week."

Five pence a day! Such a sum amazed Garth. In all his working days, he had never earned a penny.

Garth next heard the old man invite his friend to his home for a night's lodging. Garth was startled. This lodge, then, was just for work, meals, meetings, and afternoon naps. If this were true the building would be closed and locked when the men rose from their rest. Garth would be penned inside with nothing to fill his aching stomach but a drop of ale that might be left in someone's mug.

He knew now that he must leave with the others when their rest ended. In the yard below, he saw young men mixing mortar and carrying stone. Now that he had a stone mason's grey tunic and a big heavy hood to hide his hair, he too could fill his arms with stones and carry them about as though he were a worker. He was as tall and strong as most of them. He felt inside his clothes to be certain his chisel was fastened securely. Perhaps if he were wary he could slip the pruning hook and his bundle from their hiding place.

The rest period was short and a bell roused the workers. No time was wasted. When the masons clamoured down the stairway, Garth followed behind them. As he bolted through the door, a mason grabbed him by the shoulder.

"You must be the new portehacher," he said,

looking Garth squarely in the face. "Your rests should be taken elsewhere. This lodge is only for the masons."

Garth nodded vigorously, ready at this point to agree with any demand.

As he stepped outside, he heard Sir Robert's squire shout, "I've found the runaway villein's pruning hook and bundle!"

Most of the workmen paid little attention. Garth followed their example. But he was taut with fear, as if Hawkin's shadow had suddenly appeared from Dodding and trapped him in a black net.

The pilgrim roused himself and went to the shrieking squire's side. Garth could hear each word.

"Stop the screeching, lad," he said. "You'll only send the poor waif of a boy into deeper hiding."

The cries must have reached Sir Robert, for he soon appeared. He examined the pruning hook and then said with growing anger, "We should leave for the manor of Dodding before sundown. The boy must be found within the hour. If he has escaped, we can at least return his tool and bundle."

Garth pulled the hood far over his face. What was a portehacher? If he stood about in idle stupor, every eye would be attracted to him. If he asked a question, someone would be suspicious.

He picked up a large stone and began to carry

it to the west end of the stone yard, but the mason who had scolded him a few minutes before called, "Here, lad, take my mallet and my chisel to the smithy and have the one tightened and the other sharpened." The mason looked towards the east as he spoke, so Garth headed in that direction.

He soon heard the familiar bellows of the blacksmith and found it to be like the one in Dodding.

Boys carrying tools waited their turn with the blacksmith. They held wedges, picks, trowels, and axes, as well as chisels and mallets. The blacksmith filed and ground and reworked each tool with fine precision. These boys must be portehachers, Garth decided. He watched them carefully, determined to learn his new work well.

The boys talked and laughed with one another. One of them turned towards Garth.

"They say you're new," he said, "That you've come to take the place of the boy who died of ague. What's your name?"

"Garth."

Should he have given another name? Garth wondered. It was too late now. Besides, how would he think to answer to John or William, or even Edmund. If only he could call out to Edmund now. He felt a twinge of sadness for the portehacher who had died. Ague, with its fever and chills, was often suffered by the villagers of Dodding.

Garth's tools were soon in order and he hur-

ried back to the mason who seemed to be directing him. Sir Robert, his squire, and the pilgrim
had left the stone yard and were walking towards
the west door of the great cathedral.

Garth's mason gave quick orders.

"Take these tools inside the cathedral," he
said, "and give them to the mason working on the
border above the Prior's Door. Ask for directions
to the monks' cloisters. You'll find the door there.
Go into the cathedral through the west door, and
make haste."

For a moment Garth could not move. The joy
of finally entering the cathedral washed over him
like a flood of bright sunshine. But the terror of
following behind Sir Robert, the squire, and the
pilgrim, who were now walking in front of him,
turned his legs to stone.

❧ 14 ❧

M ake haste," the mason frowned at Garth, "or I will find another portehacher with legs that move."

Garth grabbed the tools and pulled his hood forward. He stumbled on the cobblestones, almost running into a beggar. The poor man, Garth thought, was probably on his way to ask for food at the almonry gate on the monastery grounds near the cathedral. A chilling remembrance ran through Garth's already troubled thoughts.

Hadn't Edmund been captured before that very gate begging for food? Garth's mouth watered as he imagined bread and bits of meat being ladled into the beggar's earthen bowl.

Sir Robert and his squire were ahead, the pilgrim, without the aid of either mule or villein, puffing behind them. Garth slowed his steps. He must not overtake the little man.

"If any of them turns around and recognize me," he decided, "I'll drop the tools and run." He clasped the tools against his thumping heart.

Because he could not raise his head, Garth

bumped into a stone step and almost fell to the ground. Somehow his feet held firm against the smoothness of the stone and Garth knew that he was about to enter the cathedral. He could see a towering door, outlined by layers of stone arches. Beside them were slender shafts of polished marble.

He walked through the doorway. An awesome silence suddenly swallowed up the clang of mallets, the cries of builders and the moans of beggars. The outer world receded as though a wind had swept it far away. Garth's arms hung loosely at his sides as he paused to look about with wonder.

Columns of stone rose like giant oaks, one behind the other, on either side of the nave. To Garth, the centre of this great cathedral seemed to stretch as far as the earth's rim and as high as the sky. Cushions of stone on top of each column supported row after row of pointed arches. Above these were more stone columns and more arches, and far, far above was still another sprouting of columns, topped by more pointed arches.

From the highest arches, jewelled windows of stained glass flooded light upon the people below. It splashed in pools of rubies, sapphires, emeralds, and gold. And among these highest pillars, Garth saw black-robed monks strolling from arch to arch. He threw back his head to look above the coloured windows and was astonished to see a roof of stone-ribbed vaulting that unfolded into giant fans. A bird, no larger than a speck of dust, circled among them.

What men could build at such a height? Garth
wondered. Surely God had sent His angels out of
heaven to build this.

Garth was jarred by the nudging of an elbow
in his back. It was the pilgrim. An incoming crowd
of people had pushed the two together, so close
they were like birds inside a net.

"My boy," the pilgrim whispered carefully into
Garth's ear, "you cannot hide your walk, your
manner, and your ogling eyes with new garments
and an ill-fitting hood. I've known, since I first
heard you speak and leaned against you on the
causeway, that you were a runaway peasant from
Dodding. I thought I'd take you with me on my
travels. Now I see you are better employed."

For the first time Garth looked into the round,
good-natured, kindly face of the pilgrim. He was
surprised. There was no cruelty or condescension.
Instead, the pilgrim's eyes were friendly and he
smiled warmly. Garth's fear of him ebbed away.

Before Garth could speak, the pilgrim whispered further, "Where have you been ordered
with these tools?"

"The Prior's Door." Garth barely moved his lips.

"Then follow me," the pilgrim said, "but see
that you are far behind." He paused to dip his fingers in a font of holy water and made a swift sign
of the cross. Garth did the same.

The pilgrim sauntered away from Sir Robert
and his squire, walking under one of the arches
into the south aisle beside the vast and silent nave.

Among the patches of jewelled colour, shafts of sunlight fell on the columns, across the stone floor and upon the carved stone figures of bishops and noble men and women lying stiffly on tombs along the outer wall. And protruding from stone blocks projecting from the walls were carved stone heads of bats grinning like cats. Garth almost laughed aloud when he saw them.

A traveller in knight's armour bumped against Garth. He spoke with alarm to a fellow knight beside him.

"Don't go near the choir," he warned. "The cracks in the piers below the spire grow wider every day. There is talk that the spire might fall."

Garth shivered. The end of the world would surely come if any of these massive pillars cracked and fell.

Garth looked about for the pilgrim and saw him pushing open a door against the south wall. Of course, Garth realized, it was the Prior's Door, which opened into the cloister of the monastery where the monks lived and worked. He followed the pilgrim through the door and found himself out of doors again.

Before him was a rich green square of grass with a covered passageway all around it supported by elaborately carved stone pillars. Garth began to follow the pilgrim around it. Suddenly a rush and swish of black-robed monks and chattering schoolboys entered from a nearby door and scattered in all directions. Some of them settled themselves at

desks in the library and writing room that opened
from the opposite wall onto the cloister.

A warm, bright sun shone down on everyone.
Several monks seemed to be taking their daily exer-
cise around the ambulatory. The pilgrim stopped
to chat with one of them. Garth could see that they
were friends. The pilgrim turned towards Garth,
his face flushed with the excitement of his talk.

"My boy." He placed his hand once more upon
Garth's shoulder and lowering his voice said,
"Listen to me well for I must be upon my way. Sir
Robert and his squire will never look for you here
in the monks' cloister. Stay as long as you can."

Garth listened tensely. He would remember
every word the pilgrim told him.

"If it is freedom that you seek, my boy, I wish
you well." The pilgrim's voice no longer had a
pompous ring. He spoke as one man to another.
"I believe that matters will not go well in our land
until there is freedom for every man."

Garth was shocked. Such words were dangerous to speak aloud, yet he had heard them before.
But where?

The pilgrim's eyes met Garth's. "Trust me not
to tell anyone of your whereabouts. Serve God,
who made no man better than another. And take
care that someday you might have a craft that is of
your own choosing."

He gave Garth's shoulder a final squeeze and
walked into the cathedral without a backward
glance.

🐚 **15** 🐚

Garth wanted to cry out to the pilgrim to stay with him longer. He felt a hollow, lonely ache inside him. Without a guide, Garth did not know if he could stay in this sheltered cloister. If he went into the cathedral again, would Sir Robert recognize him as easily as the pilgrim had?

In the stone yard at the north of the cathedral from which Garth had just come, the wind whipped and furled the stone dust into eddies. Here in the monks' cloister against the cathedral's thick stone southern wall, there was no wind. At least not on this day. The shining sun lay like a golden blanket over everything. Tired and hungry, Garth sat down beside a pillar. No one seemed to notice he was there.

Four young boys of the monastery school seated themselves on the stones before a door. The monk who had talked with the pilgrim stood before them. Garth listened but he could not understand. They must be speaking in Latin. Perhaps these were the boys, he thought, who had sung when Edmund was here. Edmund! How he wished that he were with him now. He would not believe that he had drowned.

Garth approached the Prior's Door and rubbed his finger gently over the carvings around it painted in bright colours. At the top was the face of a robed saint cut out of stone. Garth looked closely. Many stone-carved scenes were fitted into small stone frames. In one frame a pair of lovers kissed. They held a single cup between them. Flowing around the frames were spirals of stone stretched into long, thin, twisted strands.

Garth could not take his eyes from the door. He wished for a chisel and mallet so that he might try carving something in a small stone frame.

He was so intent on all he saw that he did not notice a tall figure standing close beside him. A deep voice boomed, "Have you brought my tools?"

Garth was so taken aback that he staggered as though he had been beaten. With shaking hands, he gave the tools to the waiting mason.

"The lad must be hungry or ill." The stone mason motioned to a monk nearby and walked away.

"I am very hungry," Garth whispered.

The monk propped him against a pillar and soon brought him a steaming bowl and a brimming mug of ale.

Garth looked at the food, expecting porridge. Instead there was a fluff of white, as if a piece of cloud had fallen into the bowl.

"It's rice with almonds," the monk said, "a special treat for the Prior, who ate with us this day."

Garth gulped the ale, but let this new food linger in his mouth. It was delicate and sweet, like petals from a honeysuckle vine.

When Garth finished, his weakness disappeared. He was ushered through the door and again entered the cathedral.

Garth carefully pulled the hood over his face and hair. Sir Robert and his squire might be nearby. He wished again that the pilgrim would appear to guide him. Walking far around the central nave, he found himself among the soaring pillars of the cathedral's north arm. The ill-fitting hood slipped again to his shoulders.

Without his hood Garth could look about more easily and he noticed on one of the pillars a large stone head. The face appeared to smile at him. Garth looked at it more closely and then he laughed aloud. A huge ear strained out from the stone head, as though to catch each word from the visitors and the monks below.

In the silence of the vast and lofty hallway, Garth's laughter echoed loud and hollow. A knight nearby drew back and shook his head. Garth had no time to collect his wits. He heard the voice of Sir Robert nearby.

"There! Runaway!"

Garth jerked the hood over his head. He bent low and slipped into the darkest corridor. Then he ran, jostling worshippers this way and that, holding his woollen mantle close around him. At

one place in the wall he came upon some narrow
stairs of stone. He began to climb them, up and
up and up. He thought his lungs might burst before he reached the top. At the highest step, he
fell upon a worn stone floor and gulped for air.
Far below he heard the chanting of the monks
who had gathered for a service.

When he could breathe normally again, Garth
saw that he was lying in a pool of light. He was on
the level with the glowing, stained-glass windows.
He had reached the highest floor of the cathedral, the clerestory. He listened for footsteps on
the stairway. There was only silence. He leaned
forward cautiously to look below. His stomach
turned inside him. His head felt light. He had
never been so high above the ground.

He walked carefully along the narrow gallery,
and finding no one there wrapped his mantle
around him and sat upon the worn stone passage.
Exhaustion overcame him, and within minutes he
was asleep.

Garth stirred in his sleep. A faint singing hummed
in his ears. He opened his eyes, but he could see
nothing. Had he been blinded? Where was he? He
turned towards the sound of the music and far, far
below he could see its source. Specks of light, like
candles, flickered faintly in the blackness.

Garth stretched out his hand and touched the
hard stone floor. Now he remembered. He was
high above the nave of the great cathedral of Isle.

He had fallen asleep, and now it was night. The monks were singing matins, their service two hours after midnight.

Garth shook with cold and terror. In this darkness, one false step and he could be hurled into endless space. He began to crawl slowly on his hands and knees, feeling his way until he found the stone steps. Then he went down backwards, first one knee and one hand, then the other knee and other hand. The coolness of the stone made him shiver.

After what seemed like an eternity he felt the sturdy floor of the nave. Slowly his eyes accustomed themselves to the dark and he could make out the towering columns and the tombs along the walls. The candlelight grew brighter and the chanting louder.

A silent monk strode near him. Garth shivered so violently that his teeth chattered. He hunched his shoulders and drew his cloak tightly around him.

"They must come each night, even if the air is solid ice," Garth marvelled.

The singing filled the empty caverns of the cathedral. The notes were clear and pure and echoed in the vast space. Garth stood motionless until the service ended.

Silently the monks began a processional towards a door that opened onto a flight of stairs. The darkness rolled behind them like a wave as one by one each lighted candle left the cathedral.

"I must leave too," Garth realized in panic.

To be the only breathing soul inside the nave in total darkness was a thought too frightening to contemplate. His only company would be the motionless stone figures above the tombs and the smiling head with the outstretched ear. Garth pushed against a door that opened into the monks' cloister. He stumbled and fell headlong onto the soft clipped grass, wet with dew.

Because the moon was wrapped in clouds, it was almost as dark outside the cathedral as within. Garth stood up and began to feel his way along a row of buildings beyond the cloister that bordered on a narrow path. The buildings ended and his feet touched damp grass.

There was the earthy smell of a meadow and the bubbling sound of a shallow brook. If the place had been Dodding, Garth would have spread his mantle here and finished his night's rest. But not far away he could see the outline of a wall and what appeared to be an opening beside a heavy gate. He ran towards it and squeezed through.

Outside the wall, the houses of the town crouched along the road, asleep under their mantles of thatch. Here and there a dog howled, and a cat silently brushed against Garth's legs.

Using the wall for his guide, Garth found himself before too long among the stones and slabs of marble in the stone yard. He crawled beneath a sheltering rock and fell upon the ground. He felt a peace and comfort in this yard.

He would have slept at once if only there had not been a new throbbing ache in his head.

"A bother and a nuisance," thought Garth. "Perhaps I need some food again. But that will have to wait until the morning."

❦ 16 ❦

The pain still pounded in Garth's head when he woke at early dawn. A chill wind made him shiver even inside his woollen mantle.

He peered around his sheltering rock and saw some stone workers coming to their lodge. But of greater interest to him at that moment was a plump man with a wooden ladle and a pot standing in the doorway of the lodge. He appeared to be the cook.

Garth wished for yesterday's warm sun. Then he remembered that if Sir Robert were still in Isle, it was best to have a murky sky.

With his shivering, the pain in his head, and a new weakness in his legs that made him totter when he tried to stand, Garth felt sick and disheartened.

"You're a hungry-looking one," the cook said before Garth could open his mouth. "It's good that I saw you today and not tomorrow. In another day, you might be dying of starvation."

Without another word he handed Garth some dried herring and a mug of ale. Garth ate and drank in gulps. He thanked the good man and walked quickly to the masons' lodge. The food lifted his spirits.

At the doorway, the mason who had given him work the day before handed him two mallets. "Take them with all haste to the Master Mason along the north wall."

Garth balanced the heavy mallets over his shoulder and hurried towards the wall.

A hoarse cry rose ahead of him, cutting through the surging wind. Garth ran towards it.

He saw above him a man clutching a platform lashed together with ropes. Suddenly he lost his grip and began hurtling awkwardly through space. Luckily, he splashed into a pool of water. High above, however, on the platform where the man had been standing, a heavy stone swung wildly to and fro. It hung from a hoisting rope wound around a great wheel. The rope was fraying above the stone's weight. It would soon rip and the stone would plunge onto the fallen man below, who seemed to be injured and unable to move.

The deep voice of Master Mason John shouted an order. His blue hood, darting here and there, became the object on which all eyes focused.

"Grab Thomas. Pull him to safety!" he cried.

"Thomas!" Garth raced towards the fallen man. He could not believe his eyes. It was Thomas the stone carver. Garth grabbed his arm and pulled him from the pool of water.

The blue hood of the Master Mason moved beneath the swinging stone.

"It will fall into this space!" he shouted again. "Stand behind me."

And then the frayed rope snapped. A shaking thud into the pool sent sprays of water onto the faces of all nearby. But the heavy stone hit no one. Master Mason John's swift action and Garth's rescue had meant the difference between life and death for Thomas. A mixed look of fear and gratitude showed on the mud-covered faces of all the workers.

Garth's legs began to shake. A sharp pain shot through him. For some unexplained reason he could not focus on the men who gathered around him. Faces blurred and then began to turn in circles. Strong hands gripped Garth's body and then pressed against his aching head.

"The boy is sick," Garth heard a voice say. "He has no boils on his skin, but his body burns with fever. It could be the Fenland ague. We must take him to the infirmary with Thomas. . . .The boy is a brave lad."

Garth felt himself being lifted from the ground. He tried to look about him, but the light faded away and he tumbled into darkness.

Strange days of shadows became Garth's world. Then there were nights of blackness so thick he could not see before him when he woke with thirst. His swollen tongue could form no words, but when he grew feverish, a cool, firm hand stroked his throbbing head and water was poured on his tongue and lips.

Once Garth heard a gentle woman's voice say, "Mix the boy some poppy-head tea." Then another woman's voice argued, "It's tea from the willow bark he needs, to cut down the ague fever."

Chills shook Garth, and after them a fever pierced his head like a branding iron and he thought he might be roasting with a joint of meat at the harvest feast in Dodding. He cried for Mother and Edmund. But they didn't come.

"Hush, lad, hush," a calm, low voice broke through the heat, and again the cool, firm hand stroked his head.

Garth forced his eyes to open. Swimming before him was a lean, kindly face—Thomas! In quick succession Garth remembered the falling stone, and Thomas in the pool, his leg twisted at an odd angle. Garth sat upright from a pallet of straw.

"Your leg?"

"My leg is healing," Thomas answered. "Now rest yourself, lad, and close your eyes."

Garth fell backward. He hadn't the strength to sit up longer and the light pained his eyes when he held them open.

At last Garth woke one morning and found that the pain in his head had subsided. Even the fever had left him and his tongue was no longer swollen.

He was lying on a pallet in the corner of a large yard, and all about him were stone masons in their grey and dusty tunics. One of them near him was splitting a huge stone. Another was carving thin stone tracery for the frame of a cathedral window. Boys trotted by, carrying tools and water. And beside Garth sat Thomas with a bandaged leg.

Thomas was perched on a two-legged stool with a jagged lump of stone between his knees. His chisel was sharp and his mallet was strong and he sang a merry tune.

> Pick-a-back imps in glee
> With the wings of a bat!
> And the grin of a cat,
> Making mock at you and me,
> Sing nonny ho, nonny he,
> Oh what fools poor mortals be!

One dust-covered foot beat the time as he sang. Emerging from Thomas's stone was an imp with the grin of a cat and wings like a bat. Garth laughed.

Thomas wheeled about on his stool.

"At last you've come to your senses!" he cried.

Garth smiled at his friend. Then he grew pale.

"Edmund! I ran away with Edmund and he was lost in the Fens."

"Yes, I know," Thomas smiled.

"Am I in the masons' yard?" Garth asked with

a puzzled frown. "I thought I heard the Master Mason say I should be taken to the infirmary."

Thomas shook his head. "That was many weeks ago."

Then Thomas told Garth an unbelievable tale. For many days the two of them had been side by side in the infirmary, Thomas with his broken leg healing and Garth tossing to and fro with fever from the ague.

The monks had sometimes thought Garth would die, but Master Mason John, who seemed to have taken a liking to Garth and looked in on him often, always said, "The lad is tough and brave and sturdy and he has a goal set for himself. He will get well."

A goal? How did the Master Mason know? Had he babbled all his thoughts and tales during those days of fever? If he had, Thomas knew them too. Garth turned towards his friend with apprehension.

"What did I say, Thomas, when the fever addled my brain?"

Thomas eyed the young patient with a level gaze and said, "I'll put it to you honestly, lad. From your babblings, I learned to know your friends and foes better than I did in Dodding, but some of them I had never heard of before. There is a girl you called by the name of Mermaid." He paused, waiting for an answer, but Garth had none. Mermaid swam about in his head like some mysterious creature from another time and place.

Thomas continued, "I know how you came here and why you want to stay. In the name of good St. Benedict I will never speak a word of your tale to anyone."

Garth knew that Thomas could be trusted. His secret would be kept. But there were other worries.

"Is there news from Dodding?" Garth whispered cautiously. "And what of Hawkin and Sir Robert? And Edmund?"

Thomas shook his head. "There is word that the village of Dodding is rife with ague. Even Hawkin has taken to his pallet. I have news of no others."

Could Mother and Edmund also have the ague? Garth felt his fever might rise again inside him. He lifted his head.

"And what of the other monks in the infirmary, Thomas? Did they hear my babblings? What of Master Mason John? And who were the women I heard?"

Quickly the solemn mood of Thomas changed and his face broke into a lopsided smile.

"I was your caretaker, lad," he joked. "The monks had no time for your babblings. And don't worry your head about the Master Mason. Every mason is a free man. Our Master Mason could never wish it to be otherwise for anyone. It was his good wife and daughter Mary with the flowing raven hair who bathed your head and gave you herbs."

Flowing raven hair. Again Garth's head spun,

but he had no explanation for himself or Thomas.

In the days that followed, Garth's strength slowly returned. Thomas promised that soon he would be walking and could again return to his work as a portehacher. At night Thomas carried him to the infirmary, where he ate and slept. In the daytime he propped Garth against the wall of the masons' yard near his work.

Garth watched closely as Thomas carved. Each day more of the grinning imp emerged from the stone. Thomas explained one day to Garth that the monks usually told him what holy image he should make, but for this piece they had not given him advice. The imps, and Thomas hinted there would be more than one, would be placed in the newest part of the cathedral. They would be corbels projecting from a wall to help support the beams of the roof. Their exact size was measured and a mark made on them to show where they would be placed.

"Sometimes we need to laugh as well as pray," Thomas winked at Garth.

Garth observed carefully each incision that Thomas made—how he held his chisel and mallet, and how he used his level and his square to make his work precise.

Soon Garth began to polish chisels for the masons with ashes from a pot. Each morning Master Mason John came to the stone yard to check that no work was shoddy, that pieces of stone for windows and arches would fit perfectly in the spaces waiting for them in the cathedral. One day he came with coins to pay the workers. He counted out six shillings for each mason's weekly allowance and a much smaller amount for each portehacher.

He called the workmen's names and they walked up to him for their pay. Garth heard his own name called! "Garth, the portehacher, who worked two days before his illness and who will walk and work again, receives four pence."

Master Mason John walked to Garth's pallet and placed the coins in his open hand.

Garth looked at them with disbelief. He felt the hardness of the metal in his palm. He had never held a coin, and these were his for work that he had done. He felt a lump in his throat and warm tears spilled against his cheeks.

He wanted to stand to thank the Master Mason. He gripped Thomas's shoulder and pulled himself slowly upright until he stood, shaking and wobbly.

The Master Mason said nothing, but he looked pleased. Thomas grabbed his young friend's arm.

"Now I know that you will walk again," he said.

Garth took four steps and then fell back exhausted.

❦ 17 ❦

It was winter now and most of the work had to be done inside. Many of the masons had left to find work in other places. During the daylight hours, Garth was allowed in the lodge, where he sat beside Thomas and helped with his tools. Now that he was well again, he was allowed to sleep at night in a corner of the lodge.

One morning Master Mason John called out an important announcement. "On this 19th day of February, 1322," he said, "it is good to tell you that the new chapel we have been working on has a finished foundation and two of the walls are high above the ground."

All the masons cheered.

The winter days blew cold with frost and snow and the sky became slate grey like polished ice. But now and then a sunny day arrived and the workmen moved their stones and tools outside to clear their lungs of dust.

On such days Garth managed to stay indoors and pull a small block of stone from beneath his pallet. With his own small chisel and a small mallet that he had borrowed, he was working on the carving of a simple dog-tooth moulding. He had seen other masons carve these rows of pyramidal projections, each carved into four leaves. They could be seen as ornamental mouldings in many parts of the great cathedral of Isle.

As Garth worked, the leaves became smoother and more lifelike. It was a task, however, that he had to keep secret. He had not earned the right yet to carve stone. He could not be an apprentice to a stone mason until he was a free man. There were many days left yet until his term of one year and a day away from Dodding was completed.

Each day Garth felt stronger. He began to make trips in and out of the masons' lodge to carry water and deliver small tools. Thomas worked feverishly on his imps. There were two of them now, one riding pick-a-back on top of the other, and both had monstrous grins. Thomas had also been asked by Master Mason John to carve several gargoyles since he seemed to have a special talent for weird faces.

"Gargoyles?" Garth was puzzled.

Thomas explained, pointing far above to the roofs of the cathedral.

"On the roofs, the gutters lead to gargoyles. They are stone spouts, shaped into weird monsters, that are designed to shoot the rainwater clear of the walls."

Garth secretly stored this knowledge in his head. Someday he would carve one. But he did find time each day to work on his own precious stones, which he continued to keep hidden beneath his pallet. His other prize possession—the two coins along with others he was now beginning to earn—were wrapped in a torn piece of leather and tied to his girdle.

One morning as Garth was trudging through the stone yard, slipping on the ice that glazed the puddles, he saw a small mule ambling down a nearby path. Its rider was a plump little man hunched beneath a black serge cloak. A wide black hat was perched on his head. Beside him walked a smaller figure, covered with a hood and heavy grey mantle.

"The pilgrim!" Garth shouted, running towards him, not thinking for a moment of his safety or the proper way for a mason's boy to address a man in holy garb.

The pilgrim stopped his beast and peered down at Garth.

"You're thinner, boy. I think you have been ill."

Garth nodded.

"I've come from Dodding," the pilgrim said, glancing about for anyone who might be listening, but no one was nearby, "and I'll be going back soon."

Garth's heart beat at such a rapid pace he wondered if the ague had once more come upon him.

The man had lost his jovial ways and pompous

oice and seemed intent upon making his message as brief as possible. The small figure beside him stood with lowered head, immobile as a stone.

"It's best we are not seen together," he spoke with quiet purpose. "Listen to the news I give you and then be gone.

"The Steward of Dodding, Hawkin, is ill with ague, but he plans to come for you himself when winter ends. Watch for him and hide well until he goes away."

Garth shuddered. The pilgrim spoke more kindly.

"Your mother is well and knows that you are safe. Goderic does not speak about you."

"You talked with Mother!" Garth almost shouted with excitement. "Tell me more."

"Edgar the swineherd died of ague, and William the wary one will take his place and marry Edith, the plump girl whose sister sings."

Garth laughed with happiness about the last announcement.

"But what of Edmund, the swineherd's son?" Garth's face grew sober. "I never told you, but he also hid in a cart of grain when I did and escaped from Dodding. I have not seen him since the storm in the Fens."

The pilgrim caught Garth's tunic and held him close.

"I found Edmund in the Fens. He is here beside me," he whispered. "He is travelling as my servant. Hush! Do not speak his name."

Garth looked at the small huddled figure. Joy rose in him like rising steam. To have his best friend beside him. He wanted to shout his name!

Edmund lifted his head and the two boys stared at one another. Edmund's face was thin and pinched, but his eyes sought Garth's and they were bold and glad and merry. A thick cloth hid the scar upon his head.

The pilgrim drove his mule between them.

"Listen to me, Garth," he said. "Edmund's life is in danger. He attempted to escape twice. Hawkin blames him for your disappearance."

Garth tried to speak. He started to reach for Edmund's hand.

The pilgrim broke in sharply.

"Remember what I said. You cannot speak or act as though you know each other. Tell only Thomas, for he knows the lad."

The pilgrim looked about carefully and then went on.

"Edmund will work in the monks' kitchen. They have need of such a boy. Be off now, Garth, and remember all I said."

Garth ripped the piece of leather from his girdle. He poured all his coins into the pilgrim's hand. "Keep some for yourself and give the rest to Mother."

The pilgrim smiled.

"You will both be needing large amounts of wit and courage in the days ahead. May God rotect you."

The pilgrim turned to go, motioning for Edmund to prod his mule.

Edmund looked once more at Garth and winked an eye.

Garth watched them walk away. "Edmund is here," he whispered joyfully. They could not speak openly, but they could see each other now and then. And his mother was well and would soon be holding his coins in her hand.

As Garth walked back to join Thomas, he smelled a hint of spring in the air. The whole earth was rejoicing with the coming of his friend. The locks of winter were creaking open and new buds seemed ready to burst through the ice. Joy and hope. Garth felt them everywhere.

He tore into the masons' lodge in search of Thomas. The stone carver sat absorbed over the stone ear of one of his imps. Garth narrowly missed stumbling into it.

Thomas was angry.

"A masons' lodge is no place for children's games, Garth. Go out into the sun for your running."

Then he saw Garth's face, lit with a smile and flushed with excitement.

"I have something to tell you, but I can't tell you here." Garth's words stumbled as awkwardly as his feet.

"Come along," Thomas said, placing the imp carefully against the wall. "Let us go to the new chapel."

Other masons in the room scarcely notice them, for it had become a common sight to see these two together.

The news burst from Garth as soon as they were alone in the yard.

"The pilgrim is here again," Garth motioned towards the path, though there was no sign of the little man and his helper. "And he brought Edmund! He found him in the Fens. He will work in the monks' refectory . . . and Hawkin is in Dodding with the ague. He threatens to come to Isle and fetch me back."

Thomas was startled.

Garth continued talking at a rapid rate, giving Thomas all the details of his encounter with the pilgrim and Edmund.

Thomas sighed.

"It is more dangerous now with two of you. But perhaps with winter still here and Hawkin with the fever . . ."

His words trailed off unfinished.

His strong tense fingers gripped Garth's shoulder.

"Stay away from your friend, Garth. The two of you must not be seen together. Perhaps I can be a messenger between you."

He stopped abruptly among the stones and looked at Garth. A smile appeared on his face.

"You're as fit as any of the husky lads in the stone yard. It's time you took up the full tasks of a

rtehacher again. Be off with you now. Gather
p my tools in the lodge and take them to the
mithy."

Garth worked through the day with scarcely a
moment to eat or rest his legs. His thoughts were
constantly on Edmund, and he glanced often in
the direction of the cathedral, hoping to catch a
glimpse of his friend.

In the late afternoon, when gold-rimmed
clouds heralded the setting sun, Thomas sent
Garth speeding into the cathedral to find a special chisel.

Garth squeezed through a small north door
and entered the aisle of the north transept. A final
burst of sun streaked through the windows from
the high clerestory, warming the massive pillars. It
glowed on the gilded wings of the angels beneath
the delicate ribbed vaulting of the roof. Garth
caught his breath, not wanting to disturb, even by
breathing, this sudden beauty.

Near the dangerous place beneath the central
tower, Garth saw Master Mason John. He was rubbing his hands over the widening cracks in the
walls and pillars that supported it. His face was
grim. A young girl stood beside him. She stood so
still she might have been a statue carved in stone.
Her long black hair, pulled back with a chaplet of
jewels, hung over the folds of a short blue kirtle.
To Garth, her hair had the sheen of the marble
pillars on the entrance porch of the cathedral. He
wanted to call out to her. But why?

Garth could not take his eyes from the girl. He imagined carving the delicate features of her nose and chin, which she held a little high. He would have to paint her luminous dark eyes that seemed to focus just on him. He walked towards her, for he could see that the chisel Thomas wanted was propped against the cracking pillar beside her.

Garth did not know if he should speak or merely nod. As he wondered, he tripped against the chisel and fell flat before the girl. He jumped up at once. The Master Mason would surely rebuke him.

But the girl did not laugh and Master Mason John was not angry.

"Are you hurt?" the girl asked. Her dark eyes held compassion.

"It's the portehacher Garth, the one who was ill," Master Mason John explained to the girl.

Then he turned to Garth. "This is my daughter Mary. She has worried about you. She and her mother came to you once in your illness and gave you herbs."

Garth could not speak. He smiled and then ran with all his strength back through the north transept and into the stone masons' yard. It was a wonder that he had even remembered to carry the chisel with him.

He was grateful for the setting sun that announced the end of the working day. He gave the chisel to Thomas and then lay on his pallet and

ulled his wool mantle about him. He did not
wish to share his thoughts about the mysterious
girl with anyone. But why, when he closed his eyes,
did he see a mermaid?

❦ 18 ❦

Garth could find no words to describe his happiness and excitement the day after Edmund's arrival in Isle. He might see his friend today and talk with him. He might even find Mary, the Master Mason's daughter, in the cathedral again and have the courage to speak to her.

But on this morning, Thomas was in no mood to share Garth's happy mood. He had been told to put aside his carvings for the day and go at once to a small abbot's chapel at the far east end of the cathedral. It had not been fully polished and decorated, and important visitors who admired the long-deceased abbot were expected soon.

Garth noticed at once that the beautiful figures that decorated the chapel were chiselled in clunch, a soft white stone. He wished that he could try his chisel on a small piece of it.

There were hundreds of designs and small carvings above the door and over the walls. Garth could see a few blank spaces high up on the walls and one narrow space on the lower right-hand

: of the south door that had not yet been cov-
:d with a carving. He wondered if Thomas
:ight fill it with the figure of an angel that he had
carved in the stone masons' lodge.

"I must find Master Mason John," Thomas
said, interrupting Garth's thoughts. "Stay here,
Garth, and watch my tools."

He left and Garth was alone. Time stretched
on and Thomas didn't return. Garth thought of
running quickly to the monks' kitchen to see
Edmund and then remembered the warning of
Thomas that the two of them must not be seen together. He became uneasy and then restless. He
walked towards the empty space near the door,
holding his chisel and mallet. He knew what
should be carved there—a mermaid, with Mary's
face and long flowing hair.

He could not resist. Looking furtively about
him, Garth began chipping into the stone. He
quickly carved an upturned, delicate face with
long flowing hair like Mary's. The fish tail curved
towards the side to fit the space along the door.
He couldn't stop. He did not lift his head or put
down his chisel until the last fin on the tail of the
little figure was finished. He did not even hear the
sound of footsteps approaching along the cathedral's east aisle.

Thomas entered the chapel. Garth stepped
back, his hands and tunic covered with stone dust.

Thomas looked at him with alarm and disbelief. No one was allowed to carve on the walls of

the cathedral unless he had first been trained
an apprentice to a stone mason, then travelled a
a journeyman, and then had a master piece ap-
proved by the Masons' Guild. Garth knew these
strict rules.

Thomas walked close to the mermaid. Would
he insist on removing it from the wall? Garth wondered.

Garth realized the great wrong he had done.
Thomas might never speak to him again. He
might be banished from the stone yard. He did
not now what to do or say. Thomas remained
silent, but his face was grim.

Garth was ready to beg for forgiveness and
scrape off the small figure from the wall when the
entrance of a group of travellers stopped him.
They were touring the cathedral and had come to
see the small chapel.

Garth moved towards the door. As he did so
he brushed against the elegant deep blue robes of
a tall man. There was something familiar about
the cloth and the soft white fur that lined it. Garth
looked at the man's face, thin and gaunt with the
skin stretched tight against the bones. Hawkin!

Garth stared helplessly at the hard blue eyes,
the thin cruel lips, the even cut of brown hair
across the forehead. But Thomas had seen him
too, and stepping in front of Garth he pushed
him through the side door.

Garth stumbled down the corridor of the
transept and under the cracking walls of the

ntral tower. He had one thought—to seek pro-
ction in the cloisters and to find Edmund, who
must now be working in the monks' refectory. He
must be warned of Hawkin's coming.

The door into the cloister was ajar. Fortun-
ately for Garth, it was time for the monks' service
inside the choir of the cathedral, and the sheltered walk about the cloister was empty.

Garth slowed his steps. He did not want the
few servants who were about to become suspicious. He still held the mallet and the chisel that
had chipped the forbidden mermaid into the
chalk-white clunch. As if he were going about his
job as portehacher, he walked slowly through the
cloister.

Garth was certain that Hawkin had not recognized him. There had been no time. Thomas had
moved too quickly.

As Garth went towards the door leading into
the refectory where the monks ate their meals, a
surly voice issued from inside.

"Send the new boy to the fish pond at once.
There are guests just arrived from the manor of
Dodding and they expect to eat well."

There could be no other new boy but Edmund. Garth knew where to find the monastery
fish pond. He had stumbled onto it the night before his illness when he followed the monks from
their early morning service. He would meet
Edmund there. He hurried across the cloister and
then along the path beside the convent buildings.

As Garth stepped from the path onto the soft green of the meadow, he heard footsteps behind him. He knew without looking that they belonged to Edmund. Who else walked in such a short, hurried manner? The steps grew closer and a voice whispered.

"Don't turn around, Garth. Walk ahead to the storage house near the pond. It is filled with clean straw. I will fetch some fish for the cook and come back for you there."

Garth did not turn around, but spoke loudly enough for Edmund to hear.

"Hawkin has come! He is the guest from the manor of Dodding. Take care, Edmund."

"Hawkin!" Edmund's reply was a choking sob.

Garth tried not to hurry. The storage house was near and it seemed deserted at the moment. Several villeins of the Priory were gathering firewood not too far away. Their heads bobbed up and down as they talked to one another, but they would show no interest in two shabby boys walking through the meadow.

Garth slipped through the storehouse door unnoticed. The straw was light and clean and easy to tunnel through. He worked his way far back into a corner. A scratching noise gave him a fright until he felt around and found some mice trapped in an old fishing net. He decided he would free them later, when Edmund came. Right now, their presence comforted him. He must collect his miserable thoughts while he waited for his riend. At least Hawkin and his men were not likely to look for him here.

Garth knew that to try to escape from Isle now would be folly. He was acquainted with no roads but the one leading back to Dodding through the haunted, oozing Fens. He and Edmund must outwit Hawkin here.

It was almost dark before Garth heard the short, hurried steps of his friend. He crawled from the straw towards the door and called excitedly, "Here I am!"

Two shadows melted into one. The boys clasped hands and for a moment said nothing. Just being together to share their fears was to find new courage.

"I've a chunk of bread for you, Garth, and a mug of water from the pond. I've never known you not to be hungry."

The two friends laughed uneasily. Edmund went on.

"I've seen Hawkin, Garth." Edmund's hand trembled as he handed Garth the food. "It's Hawkin's body, but he has the face of a man who is ill and half mad. I saw him through the crack in the door as he came to the Prior's guest house."

Garth shivered, and not with cold. "I saw him too, Edmund. His face is sharp with bones and his eyes have ten demons inside each of them instead of just one."

This started the boys laughing again. It reminded Garth of old times in Dodding, when the two of them had plotted mischief together in the darkness of the swineherd's hut.

"I heard him talking, Garth," Edmund whispered. "He told of devils jumping all about him in the Fens, and then he said he'd find the runaway villeins from Dodding if he had to drag the Priory of Isle with a net."

Edmund paused and clasped his friend's shoulder.

"I've come to Isle and this is where I plan to stay," he said. "If Hawkin takes me back to Dodding, it will only be without any life inside my body."

Garth's eyes stung with tears. He was thankful it was dark.

"We'll hide here for the night, Edmund, and make plans together."

"I forgot, Garth!" Edmund jumped about and began gathering straw into his arms. "I was sent here to get fresh straw to stuff the mattress of Hawkin's bed in the guest house. I must do it while he eats his meal."

A thought flashed through Garth's head. He scrambled in the straw to the mice in the fish net and brought them squealing back to Edmund.

"Stuff these in the mattress, Edmund." Garth swung the animals playfully before him. "They should help the devils frighten Hawkin."

"That they will!" Edmund took them carefully from Garth. "I'll come back to you soon."

He scurried away towards the cloister, looking

.e a bundle of straw with two thin legs.

Garth nibbled on his bread as he watched the darkness creep upon the Priory and the great cathedral. The darkness blotted out the cathedral towers, then the cloisters, and finally the Prior's guest house where Hawkin would sleep. Edmund did not come. A sickening fear came over Garth when he thought about his friend.

At last he dozed fitfully, dreaming of mermaids caught in fishnets, screaming and wriggling.

The screaming in the dream grew louder. A confused shout of anger and alarm took its place and roused Garth. He tossed about in the straw trying to remember where he was. The clouds hid both the moon and the stars, and all was black.

Suddenly a loud voice boomed through the dark. "Devils in my bed, biting and scratching!"

"The mice!" Garth laughed aloud, forgetting for a moment the mermaid and the dangers that might be facing him and Edmund.

Torches appeared in the dark like yellow balls, and Garth heard voices. He hoped Edmund would come, but he did not. Gradually the voices dropped to a murmur. Quiet came again, and one by one the torch lights disappeared.

❦ 19 ❦

As Garth waited for Edmund to come, the storage house began to shake. There seemed to
be a roar and a crash outside, as if the waters of
the North Sea had come to pound the whole of
Isle and its cathedral. Garth raced outside in terror. Torch lights around the Prior's guest house
bobbed about frantically.

"Could it be the end of the world?" Garth
shook with cold and shock. "And a punishment
on me for carving in the cathedral?"

He wanted to be with Edmund, and not knowing what else to do he ran towards the lights.
Thick stone dust checked his breathing. The
thundering roar boiled with mounting tumult as
though straining towards a final explosion.
Screams and shouts rose and fell with the tumbling mortar.

Edmund came running from the monks' refectory. He grabbed Garth's hand and together
they ran towards the cathedral. People stumbled
from their huts, children clinging to their moth-
ers' skirts. Beggars shuffled helplessly about,

...ing thin arms into the sky as though reaching ...r help. Bewildered monks swept back and forth ...mong them, not knowing how or who to comfort.

Garth looked up from the quaking turmoil. A serene half-moon broke through the clouds and glided softly through the sky.

"It cannot be the world that's ending," Garth shouted into Edmund's ear. "The moon has not cracked or tumbled."

Edmund was not comforted. He began dragging Garth back towards the cloister.

The monks were gathered here in greater numbers. One of them cried out, "We sang matins in the choir and went to our dormitory. Then the crashing came!"

Garth and Edmund stumbled through dust and stone towards a door of the cathedral. A prancing horse behind them neighed with fright and broke into a gallop over grass and low stone barriers. The boys saw Hawkin hunched on the horse's back. He screamed and whirled his whip in circles. "Devils, devils in my bed, and now the jaws of hell have opened up!"

For a second Garth and Edmund were relieved by his departure, but they were as terrified as Hawkin. What was happening?

A heavy wind sent the two boys swaying into the cathedral. They wondered if the stained-glass windows in the high clerestory might have opened suddenly. But above them instead of beams and

slender fans of stones, was a gaping, tattered
A piece of the central tower was gone! Its smas
and broken parts were spilling into the heart
the cathedral. One of the cracked pillars had
last crumbled beneath its heavy load.

Thomas suddenly appeared between them.
His lean, kind face forced a smile.

"I thought I'd lost you, lads," he said.

"Have you forgotten the mermaid, Thomas?"
Garth blurted out.

Thomas ignored Garth's question. He held
his head and cried out in anguish, "The destruc-
tion of so much beauty! But the wreckage of the
tower is no wrathful act of God, as some might
think. The pillars were filled with rubble and
scraps of stone. They could not stand the test of
weight and years. The men who built them were
not masters of their craft. . . . That is why each
builder and each carver must learn his trade
through trial and error before testing his skill on a
great cathedral."

Garth lowered his head in shame.

Then, suddenly, Thomas smiled again. "The
Prior's chapel where your mermaid stands, Garth,
has not been touched. The repairs to our cathedral now will be vast. No one will go near or even
notice your mermaid. Still, it was wrong of you to
do it."

"I have carved something in stone that will last
a thousand years," Garth found himself thinking.
Where and when had he said this before?

ne roaring of falling stone began to dim, but
ble was still falling and no one could go near
view the damage or search for those who might
injured.

There was a moment of tense silence, then
the sickening crack of more stone. The booming
voice of Master Mason John cried out, "Another
pillar is going to fall. Stand back. Stand far, far
back!"

As he cried and as people stumbled backward,
Garth saw the shadowy figure of a girl with black
flowing hair run towards the cracking pillar.

"It's Mermaid!" he shouted. She must have
been searching for her father.

Garth shook himself from Edmund and
Thomas and pushed aside the monks and masons
who jostled around him. He ran to the girl.
Catching her around the waist, he pulled her
screaming towards the Master Mason. A sudden
avalanche of stone poured down . . . or was it
glass?

"They'll be killed!" Thomas screamed.

❦ 20 ❦

Darkness enveloped Garth, blacking out the tumbling stones and the faces of everyone around him.

He felt the pressure of an upward sweep like a gentle, steady, protecting wind. Then it stopped, and when he opened his eyes it was light. He saw that he was in a small room, lying on a hospital bed covered with a smooth white sheet.

His mother sat beside him, gently holding his hand. But she was dressed in a short blue skirt and a blouse with a daffodil print.

"You're going to be all right, Garth." She wiped her eyes with a handkerchief. "It seems like you've been away from us for a long, long time."

Garth shook his head, but there was no buzzing in it now. His mind was clear. He remembered everything. He had come home.

He sat up. "I *have* been away," he said. "I've been on a very long trip." He looked around his bed and saw Hawk, Ed, and Mermaid.

Hawk smiled. Garth's sight blurred for an instant. This wasn't the Hawk he had known in

133

dding. This was rule-abiding, grim, hard-working Goderic in a suit.

For a moment Garth felt his head might split open. He grabbed it tightly in both hands and closed his eyes. It seemed as if he were in Isle and Dodding again in the Middle Ages. He felt a sudden wave of gratitude that he had been there.

Then he slowly opened his eyes again and looked at each face in the room. He tried to fit together the present and the past: Hawk, Hawkin; Mermaid, Mary; Dad, Thomas; Ed, Edmund. Names and faces tumbled through his mind like pieces of a jigsaw puzzle.

He felt a strong familiar hand touch his. It was Ed. He was wearing his usual tattered jeans, but there was a clean white bandage covering the cut on his forehead. His mischievous eyes were filled with tears.

"I'm glad you're back with us again," his voice choked. "I couldn't finish the cathedral at school without you."

Mermaid stood beside him. She touched Garth's other hand.

"You saved my life, Garth," she said simply.

How lucky he was to have such friends, Garth thought.

He saw Mum and Hawk standing together at the foot of his bed. Hawk Goderich could never take the place of his father, but he would take care of Mum just as Goderic had done in Dodding.

Suddenly Garth knew that he would never forget the other place in another time, but now he had come home to stay and he was glad. He saw the chisel beside him on the bed and reached for it.

"It's true," he said in a whisper, talking to himself, "I've been linked with the past and now I have hopes for the future."